Second Edition: 2013

Cover Revision Nikki Skie © 2013

Editing by Wiley-Shinneman group

Author Photograph © Bleu Rose Studios

Reference Credit: The Time Machine. H.G. Wells. 1895

Swan Lake. Ballet op.20. Pyotr Ilyich Tchaikovsky. 1876

ISBN-10: 0985907568

ISBN-13: 978-0-9859075-6-3

Printed in the United States of America.

My
Beloved Tourniquet

a novel by

Solange nicole

MoonBeam Publishing

Houston, TX

This is for the baby with the cherubic face.

And to the husband who is perfect in every way…

And to Zuey, long live The Footage.

My heart is held captured by my own power

For I tremble with fear and it is only the first hour

Can someone tell me why?

Why do I cry behind the very shadows of my own

eyes?

— It's your blood that I need to breathe

The truth shall be unsheathed…

And my name you shall inhale and exhale

for the rest of your days

Because the fear inside of you eats away at the butterflies

— And I know that you are determined to love me

Even if it's 'til the death of you

My one and only beloved

Till the End of Time

Queen Dee

Part One

Chapter 1

The rain doesn't help Helen's loneliness. She sips absently at her latte staring out the window of the "Kaffe" coffee shop. Helen looks up in time only to then regret it. A couple, tall, beautiful, and in love walks in and sits at a nearby table. She tries to block out the woman's giggling and sighing. Why didn't she just stay home? She knows why. Working on her term paper had given her a hankering for a caramel macchiato latté. Watching the couple, she silently wishes she had just cleaned out her damn coffee pot.

Slowly, the man lifts his hand towards the woman's ear and tucks back her soft hair. He leans in and whispers, and she wilts against him. His fingers caress the nape of her neck. A corresponding shiver from the woman follows all the way down her backside.

Entranced, Helen watches them closely. She absently shifts her legs beneath the table. Her eyes catch the woman's sighs as he begins to trace her neck line with his lips. And with his free hand, he grasps her hair gently pulling her closer. Helen sighs restlessly at the couple and their shamelessness.

Just as Helen reaches her breaking point, the flushed couple take their leave. "No guess as to what they're about to do." Helen grumbles into her cupped hand. She sighs and unclenches. She should've stayed home. No. That did more for her love life than her double "A" nightly companion. Pondering over the battery life, Helen leaves to go finish her paper. Maybe there'll be enough for when she's done. Helen hurries past the lunch crowd.

9

In the corner of the shop, a shadowed figure sat watching Helen watch the couple. The eyes of the pale stranger catching every sigh and embarrassed shift she would make. His curiosity rose as she suddenly departed after the couple. He sits there now, stirring his black coffee wondering if he'll ever see the dark haired beauty again. Taking a sip, Carmen mulls over just what they would do if they were ever to meet.

Helen huffs behind her closing door. Term paper, she thought. Right, like I'll ever be able to focus enough for that. She drops her bag down on the mahogany desk and plops in the nearby chair. Swatting away a week's worth of junk and take out, she lets out a depressing sigh. She's going to get fat sooner or later if she keeps this habit up. With her keyboard now free she brings up her paper. Cautiously she tries to pick up where she left off.

There was a guy in the corner of the coffee shop. He had such strange eyes... Helen snaps out of her reverie to hear the phone ringing.

"Hello?" Ugh, mom. "Yes mother, I'm fine. I'm sure he's fine too." Wherever he is, she gripes. Her mood sours. "Yeah mom, Happy Valentine's Day to you too." She hangs up and lets it drop to the floor.

Ignoring her paper, she slides her face in her hands surrendering to her depression. Memories of the heart ache flood her mind.

Her break up three months ago was ugly. She practically worshipped the ground he walked. And yet, Helen found him cheating the day she thought he was proposing to her.

10

Pain ripples through her hollowed chest as another memory fades into view.

They had been together for four years. So, naturally Helen thought they were going to get married. She thought that his lateness that evening was just him planning the proposal out. Jumping the gun she called her mother and girlfriends telling them the anticipated news.

But when the clock hit 8:30pm, Helen started to worry. He was usually home from work by five, the latest six. Maybe he got into an accident and couldn't reach her? Or even worse killed! She thought of everything but the obvious. Helen was too in love with love to realize Chad had stopped paying any attention to her, and had begun to look elsewhere.

With a snap decision she left their apartment to go looking for him. Helen searched two ring stores around the block and the local pawn shop across the street from her apartment.

Panicking, she called his mother first. "I thought he was with you Helen." After she hung up she went through her cell trying to reach anyone and everyone who would help. It was Chad's best friend that answered her call. As it rang, Helen headed back across the street to the complex.

"Uh, Chad? He's… out."

"Out? Out where? And why couldn't he tell me? We're supposed to be getting married—"Helen's brisk pace had begun to slow.

"Uh I don't think that's going to happen. . ." Helen stopped short at that. "Why?"

"Because he's... at the Ritz. . ." The friend trailed off. The implication thickened in the silence.

"Wait wh- wh- why? He was supposed to propro—"Her voice died in the dawning realization. Her eyes widened in denial. Rain drops threatened to redden her already brimming eyes.

"Don't tell him I told you, K?" He nervously added.

Still dazed, Helen numbly assented and pulled the phone from her ear. As if awakening from a stupor she sprinted down the street and around the corner. How far was the hotel from their apartment? A couple of blocks, she told herself. Racing toward the horrible truth and trying to outrun her confused mind, Helen sputtered and huffed.

She'd never forget the way the sign blazed, red and sinister in the drizzling rain. She entered the Ritz Hotel with a determined yet slippery stride. She was so consumed by her search that she didn't hear the clerk. That's when he repeated his question for a third time.

"What?" She blinked at him.

"Do you want to make a reservation?" The young man's gaze took in her drenched clothes and crazed look. His suspicion calmed as Helen finally came around.

"Uhm—no. No. I need a new key." She lied adding a brilliant smile. She moved closer to the desk and leaned forward. "You see my husband and I went for a walk around the corner to shop, and I left my key in the room."

She eyed the clerk to see if he was buying it. She continued, "Chad's still out you see and I came back because I forgot my purse. I told him to hold our place in line."

She waited for him to respond. When he didn't, "You can check the reservation under Chad Couchon." Helen jabbed her finger at the monitor he was standing in front of. Slowly, the clerk lowered his eyes from hers to the screen. Chad's reservation appeared.

"Well here we are room 639. Here you go and," he stared her down once more," try not to lose this one." Helen gave a nervous laugh and hurried past him.

Key in hand, she started for the elevator. Helen noted that Chad never took her anywhere like this. She pushed past the thought and pressed level six. Now that she was here and on her way up, what should she do next? Her thoughts were interrupted as the doors swung open to a small family.

Helen fumbled with the room key as she slunk into a corner away from the happy trio. She envied them and their happy anticipation of the indoor pool. The little boy bounced about in a floating device that covered his chubby body.

Eyeing the parents, Helen caught them sneaking a kiss. She blushed as she looked away. Awashed with shame, Helen felt herself ache in strange places. Relief flooded as the elevator doors opened to her floor. She scurried past the couple and onto the velveteen carpet.

Two signs on the wall across the way indicated left was rooms 620-629 and to the right 630-639. Following the right, Helen traced the swirls with her fingers. Numbing herself with the rose blooms in orange and red that sprayed across the wallpaper. The numbers dwindled down until she stood in front of 639. Absently, she scanned the key card and turned the handle.

Lights dim, curtains drawn, and a wave of humidity greeted Helen in the doorway. Her eyes vacantly swept across the room. A kitchenette and a living area sat unused in the dark. Her ears pricked at the unmistakable sound of human voices further in the suite.

Each leaden step brought her closer to what she knew to be the bedroom. Standing in front of the door Helen hesitated. The sounds were coming from behind it. Her hand quivered as it reached for the knob. With the last of her resolve she let the door swing open.

Her heart caved as the scene unfolded. Stunned in place, she gawked at her respective fiancé ravishing a voluptuous blond. The sounds she heard petrified her further.

Chad thrusting atop of the woman, his head lolling with the undulation of the harlot's hips. Her moaning enticing him to drive harder and deeper within her.

Tears sprang to Helen's eyes as she watched Chad grabbed a hold of the homewrecker's breasts and drooled relentlessly on them. Freeing one hand, her ex lifted the slut's supple thigh and grinded deeper smacking the head board hard against the wall. Her moans escalated as he drilled faster, huffing and groaning himself. Letting her breasts go, he clamped his hand around the woman's neck and squeezed.

Aghast, Helen's eyes blinked back tears as a small gasp escaped her lips. Chad never did anything like that with me. She never knew he could make noises like that either. Disgust rolled in waves with grief and guilt as Helen watched the wretched lovers collapse in sweaty ecstasy.

Satisfied, Chad rolled off the slut and looked up to see his plain girlfriend standing in the doorway. Confusion gave way to shock, which turned to horror as he read her face. She had seen everything.

Their eyes locked in a stunned gaze while no one dared move. It took the blond, who propped herself up, to rouse them from their daze. Following her partner's gaze she looked toward the bedroom door.

"Who's she?" The woman asked bitingly. Both Helen and Chad broke their gaze and Helen bursted out the door. Chad sprung out of bed guiltily trailing after her. The other woman loped after and caught him before he made it out the room. "Where are you going?"

"That was my girlfriend. . ." His aquiline body reddened with shame as he looked in Helen's direction.

"Why? You were going to leave her anyway." She arched her eyebrow challengingly.

"Yeah, but not like this. . ." His mind torn between the hot piece of ass holding onto him, and the girl who got away. The home wrecker turned his face towards her.

"It's done. Now we can move on with our lives. Believe me, it's better off this way." She casted a bewitching look. Chad's conscious lost the war, and he wrestled the woman back into the bed.

Helen stumbled through the cold hallway. Her tears blinded her as she tripped. She reached for the elevator and thanked God no one was inside. The piercing cry reverberated off the metal walls as Helen clutched at her sides.

This couldn't be happening. Chad was the one. Her knight in shining armor. After awhile she convinced herself she was dreaming, and the crying stopped. But when the elevator doors opened revealing the lobby, she sputtered and sobbed. Not bothering to hide her tears she slammed the card key down in front of the clerk and dragged through the revolving doors.

The young man watched as the crying beauty trudged out into the storm and without her purse. The guy wasn't stupid; he knew she wasn't looking for a purse. It was her husband. What a dick, he muttered. That girl was gorgeous, and any guy would be lucky to have her.

The clerk brought up the philanderer's reservation again. He clicked open a new window and under charges he added miscellaneous expenses to his bill. That'll teach the prick. He clicked out of the window and tried to appear bored.

Bleary eyed, Helen haphazardly ran back to the apartment. Their apartment. The thought ripped across her chest and sent her gasping off into the gutter. Steadying herself she tried to rid her mind of the images that were seared into her brain. Chad's head lolling. The sound of the headboard clanging in her mind to the sound of the pelting rain.

Helen shuddered despite the downpour falling all around her. Had she ever made him that happy? Had he ever made her that happy? Why didn't she see the signs? Was she so far gone in the fairy tale romance that she ignored Chad's needs?

She bit back the bile that rose at that question. Did he not find her attractive at all anymore? A flash of the blond floozy and Helen's hopes sank. Obviously not, her mind sneered.

Helen didn't know what to think of herself anymore. Something broke through her numb reserve and her world came crashing down around her. Everything she ever hoped for, believed in, was a lie. Clutching herself tightly she felt her self esteem sink lower and lower until it disappeared into the blackness of her sinking depression. When she made it through the door, she headed for the wine.

Helen's mind skips over to the most recent memory. It was a Tuesday when she checked her Facebook and saw the informal announcement. She had forgotten to delete Chad off her friend list and that's who had popped up. In the News Feed, his status read,

"I'M ENGAGED ANDI LOVE IT!!"

Helen's face fell as she re read the line again. This can't be happening. With a point and click the bold message erased before her, but the pain remained. Numbly, Helen stood and walked over to her kitchen. She sifted through her new vino collection until she found a merlot, uncorked it and returned to her desk.

Helen didn't miss the drinking. It didn't really ease the pain anyway, just drowned it for awhile.

After a few weeks of binge drinking Helen could think about Chad without aching. She ditched the unfinished bottles and cleaned herself up. Her college mates were happy to see her sober and bathed again.

Breathing deeply, Helen slowly surfaces from her daydreaming. Arms unclenched, head lifted, Helen returns to her paper with renewed fervor.

Can't keep her "bunny" waiting.

Chapter 2

Carmen turns on the light to the living room of his flat. He drops his mail onto the Venetian glass coffee table and moves towards his answering machine.

"You have no new messages."

He clicks off the speaker and continues down the hall to his bedroom. The halls washed with cherry wood and cashmere colored walls.

His bedroom the same as he left it: canopy bed with sheer curtains pulled open revealing a rumpled bed of silk and down. Heavy royal drapes veiling a breathtaking view of the Hudson flowing past the Palisades.

He walks into the adjoining bathroom flipping the switch. Carmen splashes his face with the icy water trying to douse his heated thoughts. The images in his head making him feverish.

Hadn't he seen her before? The library? No. The museum, perhaps? No, too random. Or had she been at that party when he was in Soho? No, only hippies and crack whores show there.

She definitely wasn't either of those. The girl from the coffee shop possessed a quiet dignity and a certain elegance he hadn't seen in any other girl.

The dark haired beauty captivated and intrigued him. The way she longed for that couple's embrace. The sad isolation and resignation from life reflecting in her pale green eyes.

She probably hadn't a clue of how beautiful she was, he mused. The curve of her pink lips. The chestnut highlights that shimmered in the setting sun. Those soft slender fingers like ivory, drumming methodically on the table. The secret strength in her swan neck which was revealed with the turn of her head.

Hours could pass and he'd still have more to say about her beauty, but it wasn't just her looks that held him. Something about the intelligent yet triste glimmer in her eyes made him want to know more.

Or was it the laundry mat? He shakes the thought. Why would a goddess deign to be in a place such as that?

Realizing he forgot his paper he heads back out down to the lobby. The elevator opens and he starts for the mail box wall. His mind slowly clouds with speculations and flashes of his idol when he almost smacks into the wall itself.

He stops abruptly and back peddles until he steps in front of his box. With paper in hand Carmen heads back towards the elevator. His paper distracts him from the dark haired woman who passes him by. Snapping quickly away from the local news, he turns to face her.

"Hey!"

The suited woman turns and smiles enticingly. Disappointment floods him as Carmen does not recognize her. The woman looks confused taking in Carmen's pout and furrowed brow. Noticing her confusion he pulls himself up and smiles courteously.

"Sorry, I thought you were someone I knew." The cougar advances clearly missing the signal.

"I could be someone you know." Her voice smoothing over in her practiced sultry tone. She encircled her beautiful prey until her hand brushed across his chest and left it there.

Carmen gives a start then quickly recovers. Taking a step back towards the elevator he waves her off. Confused, the woman advances, and forces Carmen to chuckle.

"Truly, chérie, my apologies."

He makes a quick bow and heads for the elevator missing the pout that grows steadily on her face. As the doors close on him she catches him shaking his head and smirking.

That's the hottest guy she's seen in weeks, and now there was no chance of ever getting to know those smoky grey eyes, or his pouty lips. No, she sighs, but whoever does is one lucky girl. Her mouth pulls up at a thought. He just doesn't appreciate fine wine, she shrugs and heads back for the main lobby.

At last, the term paper is finished. Helen springs from her chair and prances into the kitchen giddily. She grabs for the strawberries and sparkling grape juice. Pouring the juice into a wine glass, her mind drifts back to the mysterious shadow in the corner of the café. He did look vaguely familiar.

You hardly saw him at all her thoughts retort. Well it's true, but his build and raven black hair seems very familiar. She shakes the line of thought and places the Welch's back into the fridge.

Just my imagination. Hmmm. . . Inspired, Helen grabs her spoils and rushes for the bedroom. She reaches the door and runs her hand along the knob as she closes it.

Taking a sip of the sparkling grape, she eyes her rumpled sheets. Tapping a finger on her glass Helen lets her mind wander back to the man in the corner. His eyes lingering on her body drinking her in. Those cool quick silver eyes. Remembering her strawberries she quickly glances at her plate and walks over to her bedside. She picks one up and turns it over in her hand. The image of her being fed the very fruit makes her gasp. Helen blushes. In spite of herself she looks about her empty room. What she thought to find she didn't know. Someone to be watching?

Toying with the fruit at her lip she continues her search. She squints in consternation wondering what she is looking for until it dawns on her. She giggles as she turns over to the pillow next to her. Her hand slips out revealing the aide. Sighing she holds up to inspect it as she bites into the berry.

Her shoulders slump as she realizes just how lonely she's become. Easing back onto the headboard she lets the toy lay by her side. Frustrated she chomps the rest of the strawberry down. She licks her fingers and turns for another when a thought strikes her that makes her halt and moan.

The dark haired man caressing his own toned body looking at her with intense desire. Helen gasps at the sheer sensuality of it but gushes all the same. Catching her shyness he stands and moves toward her. Helen sighs as his hand pushes through her hair and grabs hold of her.

She moans as he snakes his hand around her throat. His fingers squeeze gently and trail up along her neck. Helen can't stop her lip from quivering as she freezes at his touch. Taking in her mouth he dips down and crushes his lips with hers. Helen's body weakens with the force of the kiss and grabs hold of the hand grasping her neck.

Shocked at the raciness of her thought Helen shakes her head and reaches for her snack. This time inhibition doesn't steal the joy of enjoying the sensuality of the bite. Baring down with her teeth she sinks in slowly as her lips follow, sucking at the bursting juice.

In spite of herself and her conditional refinement, Helen moans. A luxuriating sound that stirs her passion further. The sudden erotic epiphany hastens her to reach for another delicious treat. This time, knowing what's coming, Helen draws out the sensation letting the flesh and mouthwatering juice tickle her tongue and lips. A medley of sighs and moans escape her moistened lips as Helen lets every bit of her guard down.

Her appetite strengthens as she bites into the following fruit and lets her imagination take over.

The dark man from the corner slips his hand down her side. The hand around her neck spreads and the fingers dance about her flesh. Helen moans as his caresses trail around her body. He slowly walks her backward until they press against an obliging wall. He turns her head slowly and takes in the bouquet of her skin. She sighs as his nose skims the base of her throat and back up to her ear. A gasp of surprise echoes as each of her hands are pinned up and away.

Her eyes fly open to look at the brazen man only to be met with a smoldering gaze. She wilts as it penetrates deeper and she leans in to be kissed. A smile twitches his lips as he acquiesces. Her knees give and her thighs clench together. He growls against her mouth and with his own knee forces Helen's apart.

She groans and blushes as he continues his journey at the base of her neck. This time leaving a trail of feathery kisses, quick and wet. She squirms every time he moves away and the cool air hits the moistened skin. A growl rumbles his chest as he takes in her excitement.

Craning her neck to better receive his kisses, Helen dips her pelvis into his. Her lover's excitement grips him and he clasps her arms and thrusts her quickly against the wall. The surprise gives way to a deepened arousal as her whole body shakes from the agonizing pleasure.

Helen hums smiling as her mysterious lover nestles her neck and hair. She can't believe she's gone as long as she has without knowing what this feels like. Her eyes open wide with shock and fright as the man pulls his head back and moves swiftly forward sinking his teeth into her flesh.

Chapter 3

Carmen plops down onto his leather couch with a sigh. What a day. First, the argument with his mother on Valentine's Day. Then, finding the woman he's been waiting for on the off chance of him wanting coffee. And to top it all off, a ravishing middle aged sex kitten approached him after mistaking her for his goddess. He fiddles with the paper on his coffee table which stirs up more thoughts about the mishap rendezvous. Sighing again, he heaves himself up looking to distract his mind.

On the nightstand next to his bed he finds his book, The Time Machine by H.G. Wells. He opens to the last read page and gently reclines onto his pillow. Carmen eases himself back in and finds the time traveler trudging through the lush and vibrant vegetation and flora of the future.

The Eloi come out to meet him and take him into their village. Carmen wanders through the forests as the pages turn and ends up near a river side. He peers at the little girl in the water and realizes she's drowning.

The time traveler turns to see why no one will help her, to only be met with childish apathy. In a mad dash, Carmen rushes to save her—

He snaps up when the noise gets louder. Reality seeps in as he looks about himself trying to pinpoint it. Twisting his face to the back wall, he turns to press his ear against it.

Intrigued and disgusted, he pulls away and bangs rapidly. After hollering a few lewd comments he turns back to his book in silence.

The world arrests him once more and he's back thrashing through the current trying to save the little girl who looks just like. . .

Helen jumps with a start as she hears the banging across the room. She knows she didn't cause it. Helen nervously snaps off the toy to listen. Frightened, she hears a man yelling words to the effect of "dying animal" and "put it out of its misery"; and other words that make her cheeks burn with embarrassment. In spite of herself, she chucks the object across the room, mortified.

She burrows her head deep into her pillows praying to God she never bumps into the rude hollering bastard. Rolling onto her side, she sighs in frustration.

Carmen saves the young child and is rewarded with a look of gratitude. His smile turns into a puzzle as he no longer hold the little girl, but his dark haired goddess. Absently, he walks to shore and sets her down to her feet.

"Thank you. You saved my life." Her voice like wind chimes floating upon the warm breeze. Stunned speechless at the musical lilt in her voice, Carmen simply gawks at her.

She looks at him with a bemused expression. She waits for him to speak. Instead, Carmen places his hands on her shoulders admiring the beauty of her skin in the sunlight. Even

26

in the heat of an unyielding sun, his touch sends shivers through out her body. Slowly, he caresses her smooth skin as his fascination grows. After only a few moments, Carmen instinctively melds his body with hers. His lips crush against hers instantly.

Her shock melts away as Carmen's fingers tremble through her hair. She presses her wet body closer to her mysterious savior deepening the kiss. In spite of himself, Carmen sweeps her up and moves deeper within the brush until he finds a bed of moss and ferns. Taking her gently into his arms he closes the gap between their bodies once more. As if snapping from a daze, Carmen realizes how rash he's being towards his black haired Venus. He pulls away and sits up.

"I'm so sorry. I did not mean to be so careless and get so carried away." He sits back on his heels and looks at her apologetically. His tussled hair bounces softly as he bows his head into his hands.

The soaked Madonna calmly eases herself up. "What is the matter? Do you not want me?"

"Chérie, Mon Dieu! Of course I do, but…" God only knew by the ache in his groin that he did; though that was not nearly his point.

"It's just that you had been drowning not too long ago. You must be dreadfully exhausted! And that I almost… that I was about to ravish you so quickly after such a harrowing experience… Mon Dieu! What is wrong with me?"

His Lady of the Lake presses her drying finger to his lips.

"I do indeed need your protection, Time Traveler. You have saved my life, and for that I am indebted to you." She follows coyly with a demure look from beneath her sweeping lashes. She replaces her hand seductively back on her thigh, further driving her point.

Carmen weakly smiles in reply and hooks his left arm beneath her and with his right relieves her of her rumpled clothing.

He wakes with a start as he realizes the story had gone wildly off course. He leans over the bed to find his book on the floor. His page kept. Rubbing the sleep from his eyes he glances at the clock. A half hour had passed.

Carmen looms into his bathroom groggily. The dream refuses to leave even as the icy chill of the water washes over his face. Is this ever going to let up? He highly doubts it.

The following night holds the same dream ending right before he could remove his Venus's undergarments.

Frustrated, Carmen heaves out of bed and heads for the kitchen. He stumbles distracted in the dark as the last image races through his mind. He reaches for the half open energy drink in the fridge. He chugs it with the hope its potency has kept past its expiration date. There. You couldn't have dreams if you couldn't sleep. He'd rather deal with the crash in the next morning, than take another night of that endless torture.

He waits a few more days in the same corner with the same drink in the coffee shop. His hopes of seeing his dark haired beauty are met with disappointment each time.

Stubbornly, he stays on a particular day until closing. An hour before he's set to leave, the couple from before walks in, hands clasped and giggling. With their ordered drinks they take a nearby booth. Carmen edges closer spying on the man and woman. He didn't pay attention that other day for obvious reason, but now he sits captivated.

Every gesture, every touch they make is infused with emotion and sensuality. Carmen can't take his eyes off the female. The way she swoons each time her lover strokes her hair, her ear, her neck.

Guilt eludes him as his eyes trespass their privacy. His heart aches as he witnesses the love between them. The woman's head tilts into her boyfriend's hand, letting him cradle her face. She strains to be closer as he coos and sighs into her ear. Their coffee completely ignored.

Now that's passion, Carmen observes. As the couple kisses Carmen realizes he's been sitting on edge and turns his head with a start.

The loud noise of the floor suffering the chair's sudden movement startles the couple, and they break their kiss. Eyes wide they meet each other's gaze and soften with embarrassed giggles. Grabbing their coffee they quickly head out the door snickering the whole way.

Carmen's gaze follows them until they disappear around the corner, and his eyes reluctantly fall back to his neglected latte. He downs it desperately trying to cool himself off once again. Relief gives to the embittering taste in the back of his throat. Result of letting it go cold. Carmen ignores it, hitting his cup against the garbage can with a swish. He leans back absorbed in thought.

The vision of his Aphrodite returns. He reaches for her only to watch her skip out of reach. She runs down a hallway and turns a corner. Carmen desperately follows.

Suddenly, he hears a soft peal of laughter echo from around another corner. He races towards it only to skid to a stop as it dawns on him he's back home at his apartment.

The door stands before him, expecting it to be closed he finds it slightly ajar. Another shimmer of laughter lulls him inside and down past his living room. Peering in the hallway he's met with a pool of light spilling out from his bedroom. Carmen slowly moves forward, wary of what to expect.

Standing in front of his room, he relaxes, and then melts. A vision of white. Cleopatra herself lounges languidly on Carmen's garnet linens. The sheer canopy curtains caress the bed in the zephyr. Moonlight spills through the open vanity window and pools in a spotlight on his mistress.

Her satin gown shimmering pearls. The snug fit of the dress tapers at her waist and flows out around her dainty feet. Her figure divinely silhouetted. Carmen's eyes catch every detail, missing nothing at all. He makes special note of just how wonderful her breasts look in the silk slip.

He hasn't moved an inch since he stepped through the door. Carmen was stunned by the beauty before him. His mistress reaches for him. Spell bounded he moves forward.

He snaps from the daze as he hits the edge of the bed. Unshaken, he kneels before his Goddess and pulls her feet to him. Gently, he worships each of her toes. She smiles down at him encouragingly. His hands slide up her legs as his lips follow. A slight swoon as he brings her closer to the edge.

30

Delicately, he pinches the ends of her gown and brushes it past her knees. Her creamy golden skin glints in the moonlight.

With one arm wrapping around her waist, he places himself between her thighs. His Lady gasps softly at the surprising embrace. Her hands slide through his curly tresses.

Lost in her ecstasy he can't help but delve deeper, throwing himself completely at her mercy. A soft sigh and moan escapes her lips as her back gives beneath the embrace.

Satisfied with her reply, Carmen moves her back between the pillows. Slipping the gown higher, he slowly removes his own clothing. His own excitement and rapture felt against her feverish skin...

Carmen snaps from his prolific day dream as a male voice surfaces. He gifts the barista with a glacial stare. Frightened, the boy falters back and repeats meekly, "S-s- sir, uhm—we're closing, do you mind leaving now?"

Realizing he had been gripping the table, Carmen relaxes his grip and rises. He leaves the boy another unnerving look as he storms out of the establishment. The cowed clerk looks down at the table to clean it. A small gasp leaves the teen more shaken as he notices the impression Carmen's grip left on the table surface.

That punk interrupted a good dream, Carmen bristles. Thank God though, that it didn't show just how good. A relief that puts him back in high spirits; and with it, a solid determination to find the woman of his literal dreams. His pace picks up moving him farther down the street and back to the comfort of his home.

Chapter 4

St. John's University lets out midday for the summer break. Helen steps out into the open air, grateful for the early dismissal. Her junior year had been the most grueling yet. What with her first two years being a breeze, most of her core classes came in her third year. Only one year left until she was done and out of there.

She shrugs out of her windbreaker and stuffs it into her bag. Her bare pale skin breathes in the warm sun. Her hair shimmers with a glint of chestnut as a light breeze brushes by. The tall university with its austere cross slowly fades away as Helen makes her way across the street and down the block. No over cast to stop the rays from skittering across the skyscrapers; the sun painting the grass a jade instead of its usual jungle green. *A beautiful day.*

Then why does Helen feel the urge to wrap her arms around herself? She clutches her sides as she remembers the week of sleepless nights. Insomnia can be the product of habitual cramming for finals. But that isn't it at all this time.

Helen wants to claw herself with the madness of her dreams. Already she has bruising marks from the first night. Absently, she strokes her stomach wincing as she recalls the dream.

The second night was worse than the first with the knowledge that she couldn't change the outcome. It had played the same way: Helen in a strange place, wondering where she was—and then out of nowhere the "Kaffe" guy is in front of her.

She thought about this guy once—ok maybe twice, but still. He didn't cross her mind again until the strange dream began that day.

She was nude and trying to find her clothes. Frantically, she searched around looking on the black floor. What the hell am I doing here, and naked? She questions. As the search becomes more delirious, he appears. Standing abruptly, eyes wide, Helen poorly tries to shield herself. A smoldering man smiles and steps seductively forward. Helen's enthralled, curious as to know what is going on between them.

As he approaches though, she tentatively recoils from him, suddenly afraid. What if he meant her harm? Helen wouldn't stand for that especially in a dream. Bewilderment gives way to confusion as he stops and frowns.

Instinctively, Helen beseeches him out of sudden pity. Without warning his arms fly out in front of him coaxing her to enter them. Unable to resist, Helen inches forward. She looks up at him, his face heartbreaking.

A mixture of sadness, rapture, longing, frustration, and anticipation fill his face. His arms hang in the air unable to do anything else.

His smoke eyes lighten as she closes the gap between them, and he slowly seals it wrapping his arms about her. A soft sigh steals her lips as she relishes the comfort and security of his touch. She burrows deeper, reveling in his warmth and intoxicating smell. Helen respires deeply as she feels him pull in tighter.

It didn't matter she was naked; in fact it may have made things easier. As the notion flashes through her, heat follows. Her cheeks flushed. Suddenly, she was feeling things she hadn't in months. Warmth. Excitement. Love. Security. Rapture. Peace.

The man pulls back slowly and Helen pouts. Her mood shuffles as he chucks her under the chin pointing her face up towards his. Hesitating, she waits for the dream to disappoint her.

And yet, their lips touch and Helen's heart takes off. It felt as real as the dusty air she sucked in before and rushed out after. Pure elation spread from the roots of her hair all the way down to the balls of her toes.

She could just die from the heavenliness of that kiss. She clings to him tighter, as the phenomenon begins again, deepening the affair. Her body melts against his as they both try to intertwine further. In one swift motion she's out of his arms twirling about.

Startled and then ecstatic, she feels lighter than air, laughing in spite of herself. Light hearted, she keeps spinning feeling the stress and pain strip away from her. She was surprised by how confident she felt. How alive.

Helen swings back into the protective arms. Swaying gently around, they dance in small circles. Helen turns to look into his sterling eyes and cups his face. Looking back at her, he lovingly does the same.

Then, in a flash of passion their lips move wildly, colliding against one another. Their fingers snaking through each other's hair, unable to get enough. Just as Helen lets go completely, her lover vanishes.

She blinks trying to reconcile the darkness. The light leaving with the mysterious kisser. She shivers and tears spring down her cheeks. Uprooted, Helen snaps back to her search for her clothes the only closure in the pressing blackness.

The tears spill as she tries to grasp what had happened. Not making sense of any of it she grows desperate groping in the dark. Defeated, she sits back on her knees and hears a shattering yowl rip through the air. Startled, she realizes it's her and silence settles back over her.

Clutching her arms around her chest and waist she slides out onto the cold floor. And the more she tries to make sense of it all, the more insane she drives herself. Trying to wake from the dream she begins to crawl around to wait out the frenzy. But, when it doesn't she lets out a howl and sobs.

Helen knows she was trapped. Trapped within her black loneliness. Her head spins as she tries to fight the feeling, and rushes to her feet. She runs out into the darkness hoping to find a way out of the madness.

After running for what felt like an hour, exhaustion collapses her back onto the wood. The sobs return and a crushing realization that they are empty tears, that she was then utterly hollow, flattens her completely. The weight of the blackness pushing down all around her.

Crippled by the insecurity and longing, Helen digs into her skin trying to feel something. Slowly her knees seek warmth and she tucks them under her chin wrapping her arms around them. The swaying motion of her rocking soothes her as she lets her mind slip into the inky blackness.

Helen no longer believes she is dreaming. Slowly the reality sinks in and she can feel. But the first thing she feels is the wracking pain ripping deep into a chasm within.

Her breath gives as the night reaches in spilling into her soul's chasm. Soon, Helen is no more. Her body suspended within the nothingness. Her will diminishing as her eyes droop close. Then, black.

And that's when she wakes. The first night the nightmare occurred, she dug her nails into her sides just to make sure she was alive.

She looked down to see stains of blood on the sheet. The reality of the pain and sight of the blood strangely soothed Helen, and she eventually calmed down. Sitting up and blinking she felt as though she had been drowning. Air never felt sweeter as she drew in a deep breath. As she exhaled she remembered the sinking feeling in her heart. It hadn't left. She clawed at her chest trying to relieve the heaviness of her heart.

The fog finally recessed when she bled from her breast. Fully awake Helen jerked at the sheet beneath her and tried to staunch the bleeding. The ruby droplets absorbed by the pitiful tourniquet.

Regaining her senses, Helen made note that she probably wouldn't need to wash the blood out of her black Egyptian cotton. With finals that week, she hardly felt pressed to do laundry anytime soon.

Surfacing from the depths of her mind, Helen wanders home mulling over her summer plans. She's probably just going to read and watch movies again. Sense and Sensibility sounds good just about now. Jane Austen always hits the spot when there's nothing else to do. Already, Helen can feel the pull of the turn of the 19th century romance. What better way to kick it off than with some English tea? She cuts off her street and heads back towards the college, and makes her way to Kaffe.

Even as she walks through the door she can feel the eyes of the pale figure in the corner. Unnerved, she slowly makes her way to the line by the counter. Fumbling with her money, she waits to order her Earl Grey.

Carmen perks up from his sad coffee as he sees wisps of dark strands flowing in the wind. When he realizes that the owner of the dark hair is his mistress he absently brushes himself off. As she walks through the door, his eyes follow her, transfixed. Yet she seems oblivious of him. Now as she stands in line, his heart melts, as she absently plays with her hair. Before she can order her coffee, Carmen practically jumps from his seat to greet her.

Eyeing the strange guy in the corner through her hair, Helen pretends to fidget. Her eyes widen as the silver eyed beauty abruptly stands. *Oh. My. God!* She panics wondering if he caught her staring and was coming to confront her. Why couldn't he just yell something or stare her down like any other normal person?

Without breaking cover, she turns her head back to the menu as he comes closer. Why couldn't this geek hurry up with her tea? She waits by the side of the counter fidgeting. Idly, she watches the barista fumble with the hot water.

Carmen slowly advances, unsure of how to approach his unapproachable Goddess. He stops short as she moves away from the counter, but continues when he sees her make room for the next customer. So considerate, he aches.

Damn, the guy looks more determined, almost mad. Or was that pain? *Stupid dreams*, she swears beneath her breath as he suddenly clears his throat. The dude's clearly piqued about her psychotic staring.

Carmen didn't know whether to just say hello, or tap her lightly, so he panicked and did the first thing that came to mind. A cough. Ok, so it's not the smoothest intro but it works.

The woman reluctantly turns to face him. Her eyes tear away from the scared barista steaming her drink. Her eyes wide like a doe's. Carmen sucks in his breath. She's excruciatingly beautiful this close.

Oh no, she thought. This guy's more pissed than she thought. Watching him suck in a sharp breath between his teeth, she inwardly cringes bracing herself. When he doesn't say anything, Helen puzzles. Relaxing, she drops her panic and knits her brows impatiently.

What is his deal? Suddenly, Helen doesn't think he's confronting her anymore. A little creeped out her fingers reach for the hot reassurance of her Earl Grey. With renewed confidence she turns to face him again. After all, he is hot.

In one fluid motion his Lady sweeps her cup off the counter. His body tingles as she nonchalantly sips away. What the hell are you doing, you idiot? TALK! But it is his Lady who speaks.

38

"—can I help you?" Is all she says, but it was enough. Just like in the dream, her voice sends a tremor down his spine.

Helen watches the man quiver slightly. O..... K? She starts to walk around him and thankfully he lets her pass. With a split decision she chooses a seat and slides in by the window. There's no rush, after all what waited for her at home was a book and some candles. This seems promising, she muses.

He watches as she sits by what seems to be her favorite spot by the window. She's so graceful. His heart aches as the glittering sun catches in the chestnut once again.

Putting one foot in front of the other, he timidly makes his way toward her. She takes him in with wary eyes. Is she scared? Bashful, he completely forgot himself. I wonder what I look like to her. He stops shortly and softens his face. His hands outstretched peacefully and cautiously. Slowly, he resumes towards her.

What does this guy WANT? Hold up, he just raised his hands. Does he think I'm hostile? Bemused, Helen looks into his eyes and then quickly regrets it. Her weakened body follows in response. It is the man from her dream. Baffled she watches his lips part as they move to speak.

"I'm sorry for freezing on you like that. It's just you're so beautiful up close. I—"

Damn it. Sounding like a creeper isn't such a good idea as a first impression. Helen notes it as well but dismisses it. Flattered all the same she waits for him to continue. A giggle threatens to bubble up.

"It's just—

He runs a hand through his hair, and the other held in defeat. "My name is Carmen," is all he can manage.

"Helen." She nods in acknowledgement.

Her eyes trace his smiling lips and follow his hands as they dig into his pockets. He rocks back on his heels uncertain how to continue. Think, stupid. But he comes up short.

"Please, do be seated." Helen gestures across from her. She notes the rising blush as he accepts her invitation. Carmen folds and unfolds his hands looking around to find some inspiration. He sticks with what's right in front of him. He points at her cup.

"So...whatya drinkin?" He chuckles nervously at the anticlimactic question. *"Would you marry me?"* seems a bit more accurate. *"May I lie at your feet?"* was another.

He sits hoping that she feels more at ease with the modern day speech he was using. Or would she like the way he really spoke? He didn't dare wish to find out right now.

"Oh, uh, Earl Grey, English tea." She sips from it. She eyes him appreciatively. He'd be hotter if he spoke like Mr. Darcy. After all that's who he reminds her of. But you take what you're given. She isn't about to pry open this gift horse's mouth.

"Oh," thoroughly surprised, "You like that kind of stuff huh?" He nods. God, I sound like such a cad. He shakes off the discouragement to catch what she's saying.

40

"Yes, it's my last day of school and I had an urge for some tea and Jane Austen."

Her mouth snaps shut. *Damn, I sound like a lesbian.* She looks out into the street hoping to erase the last few seconds. The depressing sight of cramped buildings and cars passing by doesn't help. Why the hell is she basically telling him her life story anyway?

God, he thought, *beautiful and well read.* But wait, did she say high school? "Where do you go to school?" Carmen hesitates. Relief floods him as she answers.

"St. John's University, I'm going into my senior year." She did it again! Carmen grins, legal and educated. Score. Helen nervously sips her cooling tea and clears her throat.

"So what about you, what do you do?"

"I—uh," how could he put this? Would she reject him if he didn't work for a living? That he fiddled around with the violin and piano? Drew and painted when he felt like it, and walked the dangerous city streets at night?

Lie, he thought. His turn to awkwardly clear his throat. "I have an inheritance that I continually invest." Well that's sort of the truth. The questionable inheritance is stored in a vault in his home country, with a side portfolio sitting on a few million.

He needn't worry about its performance taking a turn; he had more than enough for five retirements over. Sensibly though he chose a small flat to live in that was surprisingly cheap. Well, for New York anyway.

Helen nods. Who the hell is this guy? "So what's your highest performing stock?"

"Well, I'd have to say my ETF's in financing. I'm in a short position and the Market's turned its back on financials." Carmen studies her reaction, but she nods understanding perfectly. She even manages an impressed look.

Helen hopes that he's buying her response. She could only pick out a few words she understood, the rest was Greek. Yet he buys it all the same. She tries to replay his words back, mulling them over trying to find something to add. That's the longest speech he's made yet.

And in his going-ons she noticed his speech had run smoother than before. Puzzled she inquires, "Where are you from? It can't be from around here, and I can't quite place your accent..." Her eyes squint as suspicion slowly surfaces.

Oh, shit. He sits back in his seat. People didn't ask him that. They were usually so dazzled by his looks, they didn't see (or hear) much else. "I'm from France. My accent is a tad muddled because I've been in America for so long."

"—How long?"

"Uh, well a few years." Her eyes tighten at the vagueness of his reply.

He sighs, "Ok, look. My folks died a few years back; I was an only child and had no other real family. I have an aunt and uncle but they moved to the country. I was left on my own.

42

"So in my rebellious grief, I moved to America to forget who I was. I don't like to think about it, let alone talk about it. I'm sorry." His mind fights off the memories as he watches her face fall into compassion. He's relieved that she buys the relative truth.

"I assure you, with how well I'm doing for myself now, there's no need for pity."

Helen chews her lip, chastened. She looks away again at the clerk who keeps giving Carmen wary looks. Her eyebrow lifts as she turns to the man in front of her.

"What's his deal?" She gestures towards the boy. Carmen follows her gaze. Relief turns to agitation as he spots the guy who woke him from his dream.

"Let's just say he made the mistake of disturbing me the other night." Helen turns to him as he makes a gruff sound. Wait, did he just turn red?

Desperate to change the subject, Carmen blushes. "So what about you? What are you going to do, college girl?" He turns the tables on her.

Bringing her up short, Helen hesitates. "Uhm, well I'm majoring in Child Psychology, but, I may not pursue the psych part. Maybe just get certified to become an elementary teacher...

"But if I can't do that, do what my mom does. She's a shrink; but I would help kids instead..." She trails off gauging his expression. Leary, she toys with the cup's lid waiting on him to make the next move. He rakes a hand through his curls once again.

43

Damn, his girl was deep. Well not *his* girl. "Wow, that's intense." She seems to have more going for her than he does. The thought deflates him, his features contorting into a passing grimace.

Helen watches Carmen's emotions flicker across his face. *What is he thinking about? Why am I still here?*

Making one last attempt at a halfway decent conversation, Carmen shifts in his seat. "So your mom's a shrink…?" Helen nods, awkwardly straightening up as well.

"Yeah, she's a psychiatrist for the New York State Psychiatric Institute, on Riverside."

Her hair curtains her face as the embarrassment sets in. The glossy wall blocking his view of her reddening face. Carmen's eyes widen as he slowly eases back against the booth. The unexpected awkwardness setting in.

"Well your mother sounds very accomplished, chérie. Did you always have your heart set on psychology or…?"

She perks up at the encouragement. Her shame and embarrassment falling at the wayside.

"No, actually." Her eyes grow wistful as she really thinks back. Their attention draws to the red of the setting sun. Her admirer leans closer anticipating her answer.

Noticing his intent gaze, she snaps forward sheepishly. Tucking a strand behind her ear, she begins again. "I started out wanting to be a fairy princess. I know silly right?" Her hand waves dismissively. Why the hell did she just say that?

44

Carmen catches the faintest rose in her cheeks as she tries to blow off the seemingly childish aspiration.

"No, go on please, chérie. It sounds so wonderful to dream so freely."

Warmth spreads across his face as he grabs her hand. They both look down to see Carmen's hand stroking hers. Helen's gaze lifts to find Carmen staring, almost marveling at her.

As their eyes lock, they both instantly freeze. Heat blisters through Helen's body. Overcome she drops his gaze and swiftly releases her hand.

His hands begin to sting, his heart plummeting at the emptiness. It felt so good to have her trusting warmth in the palm of his hands. It was a little arousing as well, but now he feels guilty for even owning to it.

To play it off, he folds his hands in front of him, like nothing's happened. His Venus follows suit tucking a phantom strand.

"As I got older, I thought about being a ballet dancer." Her face falls a bit, bitterly remembering her feeble dream.

A young girl with bright eyes and a lavender leotard and toe shoes ready to dance. Small Helen twirls and arabesques. The little girl leaps away as the vision fades out of view in Carmen's mind.

Shaking the memory, she looks over to her new acquaintance. Helen hesitates, catching a glimmer of compassion in his eyes. She doesn't understand why it's there. She hadn't said anything to cause that, did she?

"That's so sad." Carmen's eyes glisten. He feels for the little girl lost in her eyes.

She's unnerved by the forthcoming compassion from a perfect stranger. There wasn't much love in her life, so it was new when she saw it now in his eyes.

"Yeah well..." Helen pulls herself together in spite of the sudden heaviness of the atmosphere. She flashes a smile hoping to fool him. "It was a long time ago." She brushes the subject away with the flip of her hand.

"Yes," his heart abates as he realizes how quickly she had shut him out, "Though it seems you've still come into your own with a passion for children." He manages a half smile.

"Yes, I adore children." A glimmer of his Goddess comes back as Helen smiles. The brightening of her aura warms him. The cheery dimples and rosy blush bringing back the earlier ache.

As much as she adores children, Helen knows her heart wasn't truly in psychology. All the wishing in the world couldn't make her graceful, tall, talented, or beautiful. She chose her major because she knew that with just a word to her mother, she would have a job in months. It gave her security that dancing never did. Helen blinks back the sad truth as a few tears threaten her makeup.

Dejectedly, she looks to Carmen for something— assurance, understanding, she didn't know. But when all she's

46

met with is the disappointing puppy dog eyes, she readies herself to leave.

"Wait!"

She stops and gawks at him. Carmen hesitates, retracting his hand back to his side. What am I doing? She obviously wants nothing more to do with him. Why won't he let her leave then?

"Yes—?"
"C- Carmen."

"Carmen. It's been a pleasure, but I really must be on my way. Please excuse me." Helen readjusts her purse and heads for the door.

"Of course," he sighs. Nervously he chafes his thighs with his hands as he watches the girl of his dreams walk out the door.

"Wait, Helen!" He starts out the café after her. His heart breaks as he catches sight of her. His crestfallen angel walking out into the darkness. Should he go after her, or has he watched too many movies? Carmen hesitates as she turns onto Murray St. On impulse he sprints after, chased by a feeling of a vague déjà vu. He slows as he comes around the corner and doesn't find her.

Out of the corner of his eye, he sees her turn down Church St. He follows more closely relief flooding as they come into view of more street lights. But curiosity sets in as she heads towards the WTC Memorial.

Carmen crosses the street matching her stride, wondering just where this woman lives. His surprise slows him as she turns onto his street, Barclay. Shock gives way to disbelief as she heads for Glenwood.

He sprints into a jog as she makes her way through the revolving glass doors, ignoring the doorman's greeting. Nice digs he muses sarcastically.

"Evening, Harry." Carmen nods to the portly doorman.

"Good evening, Mr. Bontecou." The gentleman tips his hat at the returning tenant. Carmen smiles as he passes him. His eyes peer across the marble floor to find Helen.

She reaches the elevator just as he spots her. She warily eyes that the guy from Kaffe, had followed her home. He was a stalker after all. Petrified, Helen tries to close the elevator door as he comes towards her. *What is this guy's deal?* Jamming her finger into the button, she swears under her breath as he closes in.

Carmen skids to a stop in front of the elevator door and thrusts his arm in between. Helen gasps as they close on his arm and then bounce back open. Swiftly Carmen lopes in beside her.

Standing in the corner, Helen watches the man catch his breath. Carmen notices her staring and grins at her. Startled, the girl recoils from the gesture. He rests his hands on his knees as he tries to speak. He stretches a hand out imploringly as he breaths,

48

"Look, I'm not a psycho. I promise." Too weak to cover his accent, the thick Occitan of old Marseilles slips out. Helen flinches at the sudden change in his voice.

"Who the hell are you and what do you want with me?" She deftly snatches her mace and holds it in her purse for cover. She's totally not about to be taken in by some pale silver eyed maniac. Impatiently she snaps,

"Well?"

"What I told you was true. Do you think I'm trying to hurt you?" The obvious look on her face and the hidden hand within her purse gives the affirmative. "Ok, I'm sorry." He straightens up. "But may I ask you something?"

Helen's stance falters as she weighs her response. She sharply nods her head for him to continue.

"How do you live here? And how long have you lived here?"

"That's two questions," she sniffs, but answers," You're not the only one with money. My mother helps out with the rent.

"She doesn't want me working, because it would draw attention away from my studies. I've been here since freshman year. Why, what's it to you?" She hurls back at him.

"Well I happen to live here as well. For a few years now and—" she scoffs at his vague time reply, " you look familiar and it's just interesting that all this time you lived here, in my apartment building."

"You don't own this building," she pauses wondering if he actually does, "and just because I am a college student doesn't mean I should be living on campus, or some slum of an apartment." Her gaze leveling his.

"My apologies, chérie, for being so brash in my thinking." Humbly, he makes a sweeping bow. His eyes fall on the button she pressed. "You live on the fourth floor?" A curt nod answers him.

"Well this just gets better and better." Softly he chuckles as he pulls himself up. Casually he lounges against the reflecting wall.

Slowly releasing the mace from her purse, Helen looks puzzled. "What do you mean?" Her posture softens as the earlier threat fades. Rudely he continues to laugh in reply. The doors swing open to their floor.

"Après-vous, mademoiselle."

Carmen smirks as he grandly gestures out into the hall. Helen steps past eyeing him wearily. She starts down the hallway to her left. The "stalker" following behind, his shoulders shaking with laughter.

His chortling gives way to a full on fit as she reaches her door. Her insecurity teeming, she whips around to face the creep. Her eyes pierce into his jovial gaze.

Carmen was so overcome with delirium and bewilderment that he lost himself in a fit of laughter. He hadn't laughed like this since... Sobering from the somber thought, he quiets.

Noting the pang of hurt in her eyes, he frowns. Attempting a deeper genuflection, he apologizes. "Forgive me Helen, but it seems—that we are neighbors."

Flabbergasted, her mouth pops open.

"What?!"

To validate this allegation, Carmen swiftly pulls out his key and turns to the door in front of him. The one to the right of her apartment. He turns the key and pushes it open.

"Ta da!" His French accent taking on a musical lilt. The absurdity of the cliché phrase causes his shoulders to shake. Even Helen can't stop the giggle bubbling to her lips. Seeing his Madonna giggle his heart swells, emboldening him. "Please, do come in." He sweeps his hand across the threshold.

"I don't think that's such a good idea. You might've swiped that from some poor unsuspecting business man on your way here." Carmen huffs in response.

"Chérie, why would I do such a thing? And how would I know what room this key belongs to, all in the span of three blocks? Do you really think so lowly of me?" That last question stings Carmen's eyes, the mirth in his voice completely gone.

Helen's resolve waivers as she sees the echoed expression from her dreams. But what if he disappears like in the dreams? Don't be an idiot you're awake. A small voice rebuked, are you? She pinches the back of her arm secretively, the sharp ping reassures her.

What if she never sees him again, or something weird happens tonight and he doesn't speak to her when she sees him

51

at Kaffe? What did it matter tonight? Helen makes a mental note to pick up a self help book the next time she was out. This was getting ridiculous.

Meanwhile, Carmen remarks her frosty gaze as she contemplates his entreaty. His shoulders relax as she moves to speak.

"Alright, but if you try anything I'm leaving and calling security."

Carmen nods sternly as he giddily celebrates within. Helen makes way through his door and into his hall. Her mouth falls open as she takes in the decadence inside.

"Holy—," she whispers. Carmen smiles proudly following behind. Her eyes fall over the modern kitchen then onto the wallpaper she couldn't quite name. Her fingers dance across his black leather couch taking in the shocking contrast of the white throw. "May I?" She points to his bathroom.

"Be my guest," his hand flies out towards the room. He steps away for privacy until he realizes she's just gawking at the fineries in there as well. A small whistle gives as she takes in the rich textures and crystal. She turns the light off and returns into the hallway. Her hands absently out at her sides feeling the walls as she passes them. Carmen humbly follows, his hands clasped behind his back. As they reach towards the end of the hall, he blushes.

"Is that—?" Helen timidly gestures towards the bedroom. Carmen nods slightly unsure how to take her sudden shyness.

Afraid to go any closer and touch anything, Helen looks with the regard of an admiring tourist. Carmen's respect for his love grows as she hesitates in the doorway unable to encroach upon his boudoir. He suddenly flushes as an image of her in white steals him. To hide his sudden weakness he rests against the door jam.

Helen looks over to see him lounging like a jungle cat against the wall. She jumps back recognizing the look in his eye.

Unfortunately, she backs up against the pole of his canopy. Clinging to it, she waits for Carmen to do something. He continues to stare at her, making Helen uneasy. She plops onto the bed and huffs quietly.

"Why are you looking at me like that?"

"Like what?" The sensuality of the vision slips into his voice. He lingers for a moment then languidly makes his way over to her. "Come, you must be hungry." He holds his hand out for her to grab hold.

Helen bites her lip, what the hell? What did she have to lose? She accepts his hand and lifts off the plush bed. Not letting her go, Carmen leads her to the kitchen. Since he had no need of a table in his bachelor pad, he seats her at the bar stool near the counter.

Helen readjusts herself on the chair as she watches her neighbor rummage through his kitchen. Curiosity wins her over as he begins pulling out ingredients and cookware.

"Do you mind lighting those for me?" Carmen asks over the running water.

"Excuse me?"

Carmen points a sudsy finger towards the candles around the apartment. "Please?" he pouts. She slides off the chair and looks around for a lighter. This can't be happening she rebukes giddily. But it was and right now she needed a lighter.

She inquires after where one might be to which he then gestures towards her earlier place of seating. It had been lying in front of her the whole time. Oh. More scatter brained than she originally thought she tries to shake the haunting dream and settle into her task.

One by one a flicker of light ignites from each candle. Helen smiles in spite of herself at the simple romanticism. Returning to the stool she places the lighter back on the counter.

"Merçi, ma belle fille."

Carmen smiles encouragingly as he pulls together an Italian meal. Not exactly sure what he's just said in his thick accent Helen gushes all the same.

"Wine..?"

"Oh, no thank you!"

A chill of remembrance surfaces at the mention of alcohol. She plays it off as she rests her chin on her hand, marveling at how fast this man is pulling together a meal.

This man's good: towel over his black dress shirt, one hand browning meat, the other stirring pasta and then sauce. Helen notices that she never really bothered to look at the rest of him before.

Her eyes graze over the silky texture of the dress shirt, the way the sleeves are neatly rolled up to his toned biceps; the casual yet designer blue jeans that slim all the way down to his boots. Her eyes back track as she makes her way to his rump. Wow, she breathes. Is it possible for a man to have such a gorgeous back side? Apparently, after all she's gawking at one right now.

She blinks when Carmen turns towards her with a plate of ravioli, replacing the view with a very different kind of curvature. Helen blushes as she drops her gaze and takes the plate.

Carmen turns back to the stove chuckling. Transfixed, she watches the bounce in his curls fall as his head tips forward to sneak a bit of laughter.

He couldn't believe it. This woman's been checking me out this whole time! Her cuteness makes him laugh in spite of himself. Even in the face of his first role reversal, he doesn't feel as embarrassed as she seems now.

Carmen finishes cleaning up and places his setting next to Helen. He starts digging in when Helen turns to speak.

"So where'd you get that scar? If you don't mind me asking," she adds softly.

Her neighbor rolls down his sleeves. He had forgotten about it. A deep slash across his right forearm the constant reminder of who he was, and what he never wanted to be again. Helen sees him hesitate and yank his sleeve back down. Instantly, she regrets bringing it up.

How stupid of her to point out someone's scar on the first day of meeting them. Helen strokes her hair and returns her gaze to her plate. She pops ravioli in her mouth, as he clears his throat and sits back on his stool.

"It happened when I was still in Marseilles. I got into a fight and I would've lost my life if I hadn't thrown this arm up," he raises his right arm to shield himself, "to protect myself from the blow."

He smiles at her reassuringly. Helen nervously returns it. They both resign to their meals. They chatter lightly between bites, but nothing as serious as what was just said. He absently comments to Helen's small talk, his mind somewhere else.

Memories of fighting for his life slowly creep back to Carmen. He tries to shake off his past and the vicious beauty who had tried to murder him. Some more chewing happens before another attempt at breaking the awkward silence.

"So, where do you see this going?"

Helen tries to swallow back her embarrassment. The abruptly frank question almost makes her choke. Yes it had been months since Chad, but she wasn't exactly sure if she was ready for something this intense. Flattered all the same, she tries to manage some gusto to reply.

"Uh, what do you mean?" She tries to look unruffled but he's not buying it. He turns towards her and leans in.

"Do I have the possible honor of courting you?" He smiles warmly.

56

Helen's heart melts. What was she to say? No? Her lips part as she tries to make sense of what is happening. *Ok, now I know he's gonna disappear.* Helen's face falls at her contemplation. Carmen's heart sinks as he watches his Idol frown in response to his question.

Damn it! It was the scar. "Look, I'm sorry if I've said something that upset you, my apologies truly, Helen. I would've thought with the way the evening was going that you would want—"

Helen shushes him with her slender finger. That was the first time he called her by her name like that. Stunned, Carmen's silent. All thought ceases as his mind turns to the softness of his beloved's skin against his lips.

She smiles at him, canting her head as she watches him kiss her finger. She pulls away as the finger slowly disappears into his watering mouth. Helen crimsons as a fresh bloom of heat rises. Carmen looks at her bewildered wondering what she's thinking.

"I think we should call it an evening. It was so lovely, I don't want to spoil—our first date."

She looks up demurely through her sweeping lashes. Carmen melts at her modesty. Helen makes her way off the seat and turns to look at him. Her dreamy eyed gaze meeting his. Carmen stands up and brushes off his jeans.

"Quite right, we should. We wouldn't want to 'jump the gun' as they say."

His eyes drop down to his pants as he continues to fidget with them. Regaining his composure, he looks up at her and gives a smile. The disappointment resigning to his eyes as he walks her to the door. His heavy heart hidden beneath his nonchalant exterior.

It's just-- I don't want you to disappear. Helen knows that if this all turns out to be a dream, she was going to buy a bottle of chardonnay tomorrow.

She fakes a smile as Carmen opens the door. He lets her walk out first and then follows behind. Out in the hallway they both glance at each other sheepishly and then away.

"Well, this is me," Helen chuckles pointing behind her. She slowly backs away from her dream lover, afraid to turn around. He couldn't disappear if she didn't turn around, right?

Helen's heart sinks as she realizes this isn't real, and that she's been in bed after a nice time with herself. Helen gasps at her revelation and blushes. Carmen looks up at her to see her blushing and backing away.

"Was it something I did?" The hurt spreads to his face as Helen hesitates. She shakes her head, losing the frightened stare and resuming her calm. She tucks a strand behind her ear as she quietly giggles.

"No. It's just I had a thought is all." She bites her lip in embarrassment as Carmen perks up. PLEASE don't let it be him. He moves closer eager to hear what is on her mind.

"I think I'm dreaming. I think I had a good, uhm," she fidgets with her hair as she struggles to approach the subject, "well a wonderful send off to dream land." Her eyes shift as she instantly regrets revealing such a confidence. Carmen's face puzzles and shakes his head.

58

Did this girl just admit to what I think she did? "I'm sort of lost. You think you're dreaming? Why is that? Have you dreamt of me before?" A wicked smile plays upon his lips as the idea tickles him. He eases closer to her as she backs up faltering when she hits the wall.

"Well, yes if you must know I did." A flush of crimson rises up to Helen's breast as the embarrassment takes complete hold. She honestly did not understand why answers pour out of her. Was she that desperate to be under his spell, that she willingly made one to be under? Carmen shakes his head again, and chuckles to himself.

"That's funny, 'cuz I had one of you as well."

Helen's face snaps up to scrutinize his face, but he's telling the truth. They accidentally lock gazes and Helen's face softens. Caught completely off guard, Helen drops the gaze first.

"Interesting that we both had dreams about each other," she nervously chuckles and tries to reach for her door knob to ground herself, "well in mine you disappeared, so if you'll excuse me." She turns fully towards her door to unlock it.

"In mine, we made love..." Carmen softly confesses. Helen stops fidgeting with the key and turns slowly to face her neighbor. Her mouth agape at his sudden confidence. "Well we almost did, several times." Carmen runs a hand through his hair abashed.

Catching his blush, Helen quickly shuts her mouth and smiles. She moves away from the door and stands closer to Carmen. Déjà Vu. Helen bites back her sudden panic as she faces him head on.

"That sounds lovely," she manages.

Then, Helen does something she hasn't done in a while. Her lips slowly part over her ivory teeth, pulling up at each side of her face. A smile so warm so open and bright, it changes her whole demeanor. Helen feels a new kind of warmth all throughout her body as she feels happiness for the first time in months.

Almost like she had been in a deep sleep all the while, and she was now awake, revitalized. Her heart swells with a bloom of assurance. Helen feels herself lift up and her posture straightens. Where had this girl gone? And why did she come back? Whatever the reasons, Helen didn't complain.

Carmen melts in awe as he watches his Goddess blossom right before his eyes. He doesn't fully understand what's going on but he isn't about to question it.

He smiles shyly as Helen's face breaks out into a smile, beautiful as a sunrise. He fills with warmth as he watches his Beauty break out of her shell. Carmen is all but giddy when she closes the gap between them.

He wants nothing more than to sweep her up and twirl her endlessly around until they collapse breathlessly onto his bed. His eyes gleam as she speaks and he tries to contain himself as the images flash wildly through his head. Keeping his hands to himself he inches closer.

"Still think you're dreaming?" He smirks.

"No." Helen ruefully answers shaking her head.

Carmen loses control and reaches for her face and brings her closer. Cupping her face, he gently kisses her. Helen swoons as her dreams did not do this justice. The blood

60

quickens to her face as her whole body ignites from the soft kiss.

Feeling her reaction, Carmen throws himself into the embrace, succumbing to his longing. A moan meets his lips, as they both sway to the rhythmic motion of their long awaited passion.

The kiss breaks abruptly as they smack against Helen's door. Looking at each other startled, they wait for the other to disappear as the mood lifts. But as they acknowledge the ridiculousness of the fear they chuckle. Their chuckling gives way to a fit of laughter as they hold each other in the hallway.

Chagrin steals over them as they quiet down realizing the late hour, and the public disturbance they were causing. Helen shakes her head, the loose curls and wild tresses breaking free from behind her ear, and fall about her face.

Carmen bites down a moan as he watches his Venus finally let her hair down. He catches a new color, mahogany, as the fluorescent light dances across her mane.

"Well, goodnight."

Helen looks down to her keys as she pulls them from her pocket once more. She peaks up at her lover and bites her lip as she watches his face fall at the dismissal. She brushes her hair from her face to see him better.

"I had a lovely time. The best first date I've had in years." She giggles at her own corniness.

Carmen's heart deflates as his Mistress sends him home. He had been waiting such a long time for a woman like her, and here she was and she was telling him good bye.

"Chérie…"

He grabs hold of her arm but thinks better of it and lets his hand fall to his side. Helen watches his hand until it rests by his thigh. Her eyes skip across from his arm until she blushes again and snaps her gaze up. She's caught in Carmen's heartbroken gaze.

Ok now he's going to disappear. With that she unlocks her apartment and hovers in the doorway. She leans over on the balls of her toes and plants a goodnight kiss.

He grabs a hold of her hair and crushes her against him not wanting to let go. But, she unwinds his fingers from her mussed hair and pulls in a gasp of air. Holding his hands at the waist side she gifts him with a coy smile.

"Never on a first date love." The smile crooks as her neighbor's face falls. "Besides, how do I know if you're real? Or if this is all a dream?" She mocks her earlier concern.

Carmen steps closer to prove her wrong when a finger slips between them to stop his lips. She gives a few disappointed clucks and shakes her head in mock disapproval.

"Bon soir, mon amour." She whispers.

Startled Carmen steps back and she swings close the door.

"How do you know French?!" He yells baffled. Helen giggles from the other side. She leans back against the wall as she answers.

62

"I studied it in school!" She bites her lip at the hilarity of the situation. Carmen scratches his head as he paces in the hallway. Her accent was flawless for an American. Studied it in school? Carmen refuses to believe it.

"You expect me to believe that you picked up that accent from a class?"

He presses against the door with his palms on either side of the walls. Disbelief coloring his cheeks. Helen hooks a finger in her mouth as she deliberates over an answer.

It was nothing really; she was just a good student. Like any good student she took her studies very seriously studying abroad. She returned back junior year to finish the requirements for her degree. With a generous recommendation from her mother and a few of her friends, Helen landed a two year study as a freshman in a country of her choice.

"I studied abroad!" She finally admits. Carmen's head drops at the simple explanation. He lifts up off the wall and heads for his apartment. He had thought the worse. Carmen feared that she was a girl sent from his past to come haunt him in his new life in America.

A woman brought to spy on him from that trifling gang to fuck with his head until he would do whatever she wanted. And eventually, drag him back to France to reckon with Evey. He shudders at the memory of the last woman he had fallen for.

Now she was a bitch. Though she had gorgeous blond hair and a body to die for, she had a heart of steel and a soul as—come to think of it Carmen didn't think she had a soul.

All he knows is that he's glad she hasn't found him yet, and that the girl next door has no clue who that woman is. It would devastate Carmen completely if Helen wasn't the girl he thought she was.

"Goodnight!" He calls back as he walks into his place.

Helen slumps in the dark as her knight honors the dismissal. She pulls herself up and wanders deeper into her apartment. Sulking, Helen walks into the kitchen and pulls out the ice cream. She digs into the mint fudge brownie when she perks up. The softest knock floats from around the corner and into the kitchen.

Convinced it's nothing she continues to dig. Her mind goes over the events of the night, and unconsciously compares them to her nights with Chad. Giggling to herself she realizes he didn't make her smile like Carmen did.

She licks her fingers when she hears a pounding at the door. She waits to hear it again her finger hanging onto her mouth. She abandons the melting ice cream as she skids around the counter and over to answer it.

It swings open as Helen catches her breath. Her hair spills into her face. She stops dead and her wild tresses fall wistfully about her face. They reach for each other and crash into the living area. Carmen kicks the door closed as he smashes his lips into hers.

Her breath quickens rapidly as they move through the hallway leading to her bedroom. They kick off their shoes and skim off their socks holding each other's faces not wishing to part. Helen tries at the knob behind her back as Carmen presses her up against a closed room.

64

They fall in and collapse onto each other as they hit the tile floor. Carmen stretches up and flips on the light to reveal a toilet and shower. Wild laughter bursts from the couple as they reign themselves in. He stands first and turns to Helen offering a hand. The soft feel of her delicate fingers sends a shiver up his spine as he helps her to her feet.

Helen chews her lip blushing. "I should change." They both look down to see the rumpled jeans falling down and the torn blouse. Carmen reddens at his handiwork. She catches his face and he clasps his hands over hers. They chuckle.

"Ok, ok yes but where is your bedroom?"

This causes more laughter as they look around themselves. Sauntering out of the half bath, Helen points down the hall and to the right. Carmen thanks her by cupping her face and brushing his lips across hers. He walks down the hall lighter than air. His whole body glows with desire and fulfillment. Helen was bringing out all that he loved about himself and the fond memories of home.

Carmen floats into her bedroom and looks around. The neatly made bed of violet blankets and black sheets placed against the back wall. A night stand on the right holds a faux Victorian lamp.

The wall closest to him on the right holds a hand crafted dresser with her belongings askance across the top. And as Carmen stares at the wall and the scattered items a thought rises in the back of his head. *Oh, she can't be!*

Helen couldn't believe what the evening was turning into. Her chocolate ice cream was completely forgotten. She giddily snatches the white night gown off the hook from behind the door. Kicking off her jeans and throwing off her shirt, Helen then tucks in the straps of her bra into the cups. Doing a quick once over in the mirror, she brushes her teeth and splashes water on her face.

The slip shimmies over her slender body and tapers at the waist letting the rest flow about her small feet. Grabbing the red lipstick off the counter she glides it over her lips. After blotting on some tissue, she's ready.

Flipping her hair over and throwing her head back she gives her hair a quick tussle. Turning off the switch, Helen walks down the hall towards the glow of her night lamp.

Carmen can't believe his eyes as a vision of white breezes through the door. His eyes rake over her body remembering every detail of his dream: supple breasts in a drop neck line, slender curves, tapered waist, and a flowing skirt. Her hair looks ravishing in a sexy mussed look.

He gulps as his excitement grows as she turns around to close the door, revealing a breath taking backside. Hardly able to contain his excitement, he shirks out of his pants from beneath the blanket. He leaves his shirt how he messed with it earlier, unbuttoned revealing a sculpted bare chest.

Helen turns back around receiving an eyeful of the Adonis lounging in her bed. She takes a deep breath and tip toes towards him. I am definitely not dreaming. She climbs into the bed reaching him.

Carmen sits up brushing his hand through her hair and tilts her head back. Helen sighs when she feels the moist lips slip across her skin.

The warm breath and cool moisture combination titillates her further. Her body softens as the kisses deepen making their way down between her breasts.

Hands slip down the silk straps and remove her bra freeing them. She sighs, feeling the air brush against her chest. Carmen lingers on each breast, cupping them and sliding his tongue about each soft nipple. Loose strands tickle her skin as he moves to the next lavishing his mouth upon her body, suckling. Her hand springs to the back of his head pushing him closer. Her body arches beneath the embrace.

Helen exhales as the weight of the world falls away from her. Her soul splashes open lifting up to her lover's feeling every sensual embrace.

Carmen worships his Venus's bodice as he feels his heart lift, swiftly rising with the swaying melody of their souls' kiss. His own spirit embracing hers as his mouth flows down between her thighs. Her splendid legs peel apart with the gentlest nudge of his tongue.

His hand flies up to the small of her back supporting her weight. Gingerly he lies her down on the plush of the pillows. His fingers caress trailing between the valley of her breasts down her belly and upon her thigh. Helen quivers grabbing the edge of the sheets to steady herself.

Another wave of déjà vu settles over Carmen as he surrenders to the submission. Passion arrests him as he laps deeper into her lips.

His fingers return to her thighs trickling down and around until they part further. They sweep beneath her cupping her curvaceous body and lift her up. Completely overcome with rapture Helen clasps her mouth to stifle a cry of passion. Carmen stops and lies her gently back down. He smiles at her adoringly and reaches for her hand.

His eyes smolder as he pulls it away and transfixes her with his gaze. Helen gushes at the sudden flush she feels. Her eye lids flutter as his hand strokes her blushing cheek. Softly it trails to the parting of her lips and down upon her throat until it reaches down and meets Carmen's tongue.

The new sensation sends Helen's senses spiraling as her body bends and twists beneath his touch. His mouth waters as his fingers dance about in the hollow of her body.

His aching longing grows as their spirits twist and intertwine yearning for their bodies to do the same. A moan escapes from Helen's unfurled lips as her hips undulate with the swirling motion of Carmen's kiss. Rapture floods through her body and down into Carmen's mouth as she slowly peaks.

His parched soul drinks it in as he takes in Helen's ecstasy. He pulls his lips away and gently removes his fingers and leans over her.

"Do you wish me to stop?"

His voice silkily laces around Helen's ears as she drinks in his husky accent. She moistens her dry mouth as she tries to speak. Failing, she takes a deep breath and shakes her head no.

"No?" A trace of a smile in his voice.

He lowers himself down and kisses her neck. Watching her twist for more Carmen continues kissing here, licking there, as he slowly slides in between her soft legs. He cups her throat as he gingerly enters his Goddess.

He moans as his head pulls back feeling the succulent warmth of her body. His senses reel as he smoothly thrusts completely intertwined with his Venus. Helen gasps violently her body rising to meet her lover's embrace.

Time slips away as the moon spills through the valanced window and skitters across their flowing bodies. Helen's soul dances with Carmen's in the warm light as they tremble, tumbling about.

A symphony of sighs and pleasurable moans accompany the percussion of their heat. Their passion cascading in waterfalls undulating like the rise of cresting waves crashing back down to the shore of blankets only to rise again with the next wave of trembling ecstasy.

The elated chorus of pleasurable cries reaches the pinnacle with one last driving thrust and they fall softly from the Heavens and splash into the coverlets of the bed.

Their souls slowly spiral down to Earth falling peacefully to rest in each other's arms. Feeling the lasting spiritual connection, Carmen looks into Helen's eyes and gently sweeps her hair from her face. His eyes are met with a look of blossoming peace. Their lips touch as the final embrace of the evening.

Carmen pulls back to look into those eyes again. His heart leaps as he engulfs himself within those deep set green pools. Helen gazes back at him fully enraptured.

They lie there in each other's arms peacefully gazing at the other. Helen didn't know it could be like this. She had never felt such a tumultuous melody of sensations with such emotion, such grace. Tears gleam about the rim of her eyes as she looks at the man of her dreams. Carmen's eyes sting as he watches Helen cry. His frown is met with a smile as Helen caresses his chin.

Swashed with relief, Carmen releases his watery captives letting them stream down his face. Helen gifts him another teary smile and pulls his face closer giving him another kiss goodnight.

Chapter 5

Helen blinks at the morning sun as she wakes from the most heartbreaking dream. She found out her dream guy's name it was Carmen and he was a fantastic lover—

She smears the sleep from her eyes and rolls over. Something pokes her and she turns to see what it is. Ugh, she picks up her vibrator and chucks it back to the floor.

Despite her disgust Helen's grateful for the dream. It felt so real... Helen snaps up when she hears a male groan from the other side of the bed. Oh! She clasps both hands over her mouth and jumps out of bed. Standing at the foot of the bed she peeks over at the groaner and squeals softly. It wasn't a dream. Giddy, she prances about and then quickly scoots out the door.

Reaching the bathroom Helen gawks at her reflection: hair upended up over her head and in her face, straps down around her breasts—Helen squeaks and pulls the gown up. Straightening out the gown she looks back at the mirror. Great, she mutters. One of the straps' ripped. She blushes at this recalling the night before.

Bad idea, she swoons and catches herself against the sink. Her fingers grip the porcelain as a shock wave of pleasure ripples through her. She doesn't release until the fit and memory pass and she can stand again.

She clears her throat and pats down the rumpled slip regaining her composure. Quickly she brushes her teeth and combs her hair. When she's satisfied she beams at her reflection and sweeps back down the hallway.

Sun peels Carmen's eyes back and he shades them. What the hell? He doesn't recognize the room as his own and immediately sits up. Trying to recall last night he trails back to the dinner with his newly found neighbor, Helen.

He smirks at the thought of her name. How fitting, he ponders as he buttons up his shirt. Helen of Troy, the face that launched a thousand ships. Like lightning the whole night hits him.

He swears lightly as he looks around for her. Carmen gets up to look for Helen and his pants as she walks through the door. He freezes, arrested by the sight of her.

Helen gingerly opens the door wider, afraid to wake him when he's standing before her half dressed. A slow blush climbs from her breasts to her neck as he stares at her. Stepping into the room Helen hesitates before him.

Carmen watches as his Helen; his Helen, he muses, glides towards him. His eyes catch the pink flush and quickly looks away to meet her gaze. Another thought occurs to him. The sounds she made last night sounded oddly familiar... like the night he was reading his book and—

He starts with the realization that he had cursed his Beloved out. Helen looks at him confused as she watches him falter to the bed. "What's the matter?" She reaches out to comfort him.

72

"That was you," he says dazedly. Carmen falls into a funk as it sinks in even more. Helen tries to soothe his slumped shoulders but to no avail.

"What do you mean Carmen? What's wrong what did I do?" Panic threatens to steal Helen as she waits to be answered.

"You were the one I banged on the wall to. 'The beast that needed to be put out of its misery.' I swore at you." Carmen's face falls into his hands in shame.

Helen's hand recoils as if struck by the words spoken. She steps back chagrinned. She crosses her arms over her chest to cover up her embarrassment.

At last, her suspicion's confirmed. Yet to let it a sink in now with him sitting before her after last night, the affirmation takes a toll.

She numbly sits beside Carmen, as neither knows what to say or do next. She definitely feels embarrassment but not anger. How could she feel anger towards a man like him?

Calming at the sight of his mortification over her own, she lets her guard down. Deftly, Helen touches her hand to his shoulder once more.

"It's over and done with," she struggles to find the right word, "—sweetie."

"We hadn't even met each other yet." Helen swallows back the bile of shame, remembering she never wanted to meet him. Carmen eyes her from within his hands, uncertain what to make of what she's saying.

Timidly, his head lifts to meet her gaze. She smiles reassuringly in spite of her present mortification. She lets her hand fall as he continues to eye her warily.

"I feel so horrible though. That was the night I had the dream of you. If only you knew how I feel about you, you would understand—" Helen lifts at the frank admission. She looks at him with curious eyes.

"I'm sorry?"

"Yes? Did you misunderstand what I—"

"No. You said if I only knew how you felt about me." Her eyes glitter with anticipation. Carmen looks at her to see she's not upset anymore and smiles sheepishly.

"Yes, I care for you. Having you in my life lifts me from the nothingness I have been reveling in these past years, and make me feel whole. I feel like I belong," he hesitates, "with the human race. When I drink up your eyes, I see a goddess, Venus; and my Helen of Troy."

He smiles softly as he waits for the reply to bearing his soul on the morning after. He knew this wasn't what regular men did with women they found attractive. He couldn't help it though, he wasn't like most men, and she definitely wasn't like most women.

74

Helen lifts her shoulders shyly and nibbles at her lip as she considers what he said. Tucking strands behind her ear she looks at him bashfully. All traces of the confident girl gone this morning.

"Is that so?" is all she can manage to say. He nods timidly. She turns fully towards him her hands over his. Helen leans closer. "Is that all true?" Carmen gleans the fragile hope surfacing in her eyes, and cups her face.

"Chaque mot, ma chérie." Helen's face brightens at the developing trust between them. He was so sensitive and so open, how could she not fall for him? Her heart flutters as their lips meet once more. When she pulls away a rush of air fills her vacant lungs, leaving her light headed.

As her senses clear, she beams at her new love. And as casually as she can manage, she coos, "So, what's for breakfast?"

What could he say to that? Helen's breezy nonchalance throws him off guard. Hunger begins to be a bit of a problem at the mentioning of it. Carmen holds her chin and brings her closer to give her a quick peck, then heaves off the bed to make his way into the kitchen. Helen hoped she had more to offer than melted Ben & Jerry's.

Part Two

Chapter 6

The following February 14th, Helen sprays on her favorite perfume as she waits for Carmen to pick her up. Well, it's not her favorite per say, it's just the one he bought her for Christmas. She pats down her black dress in the hall bathroom and gives her hair light sprits of hair spray.

Satisfied with her reflection, Helen steps out of her hall bathroom and into the kitchen. After their usual haunt at the café, and picnics in the park, Helen liked the idea of not knowing where they were going. Aside from museum trips and local dinners, they never really needed to dress up. She thought tonight would be an exception, with their anniversary only being days away.

The door bell rings just as she finishes her second glass of sparkling grape. Setting the flute down she opens the door to find the love of her life standing before her.

Almost a year has passed and she still couldn't believe they were still together. She fought back the shadowing insecurity of her last relationship. The very sight of him in his silk white shirt and designer jeans steals her breath away. Carmen lightly smiles catching her gaze lingering on his body.

"Shall I turn around for the full view?" He turns slightly glimpsing the curve of his jeans teasingly. "Or may I come inside?"

"Huh? Oh!"

Helen crimsons as she steps out of the way for him to come inside. A sharp intake of breath sweeps past her lips as her eyes fall onto his backside. She snaps from his rump to his face as he suggests closing the door.

With a light thud she does just that, and follows Carmen into the living room where he sits gracefully. Patiently he waits for her to come around the couch as he pulls out her gift.

"Happy Valentine's Day, chérie!" He smiles encouragingly as Helen hesitates to accept it. Helen tears at the red paper to reveal an ivory colored box. She looks up at her neighbor inquisitively as she runs her hand over the gift.

"Go on, open it!

"If it's too much, think of it as a Valentine's and anniversary. Two-in-one." Carmen chuckles.

With a startled breath Helen reveals pink diamond ballerina slippers with opal stones laced on a silver chain. Tears spring to her eyes as she holds up the most beautiful gift she's ever received. A hand flies to her chest as her heart flutters about.

"Thank you," she whispers. She strokes the necklace lovingly as she watches the light catch in the diamonds. Carmen lights up as he watches Helen's tender reaction.

Her lover reaches over and cups her face to pull her close. He seals the perfect moment with a kiss and all Helen can do is cry. Pulling her in his arms Carmen wipes away the tears as he whispers in her ears.

"Juste pour vous, mon amour." His fingers trickle down her face as he caresses her cheek. Helen leans into his touch as she wonders at the gift.

"Now, ma petite fifille shall we go to lunch?" He chucks her under the chin and looks her in the eye. Gingerly she nods through her drying tears.

Plucking the gift from her hand Carmen lifts the necklace out of the box. Helen moves her hair from about her neck and he places it at the base of her throat. Carmen fastens the clasp and pats it in place.

Helen lets her hair sweep back into place as they get up to leave. She grabs her coat out of the closet and they head out the door.

"Where are we going?" She slides into her jacket as they board the elevator. Carmen turns to her slyly and flashes a brilliant smile.

"You'll see."

Helen shields her eyes as they step out into the midday sun waiting for Carmen's car to arrive. The valet pulls up in Carmen's 09 Jaguar XK Convertible and she shakes her head. She stops when her boyfriend turns around and smiles.

78

She looks nervously about her as Carmen seats her into the passenger. This car is too nice for this side of town. Helen again feels afraid of being mugged just for being in this car. The car feels more like a sleek black machine than just some auto.

She never did get used to his expensive car or the way he drove. Gaudy displays of wealth made her feel uncomfortable. They reminded her of home.

Memories of eating alone at the lavish hand carved table flash in her mind. An image of her mother, silent and aloof in her ornate den, working. Helen reading Dr. Seuss to herself in the beautiful cold blue nursery.

Her childhood went hand in hand with cold and sumptuous; immaculate and alone. She was thankful her mother was paving the way for her future, but it had been years since they sat down together. Awkward phone calls around holidays were the extent of their relationship now.

Helen eyes her boyfriend warily. Carmen just grins devilishly at the frightened girl. Without turning away from her, he revs up the engine and takes off out of the lot. Helen flies back into her seat as the car lunges forward out into the middle of lunch hour traffic. She struggles to put her seat belt on as they peel onto New York 9A North.

"Seriously, where are we going?" Carmen notes the hint of annoyance tinged with fear and slows down.

"I told you to lunch," he offers innocently. Helen glares at him with her hands folded across her chest. Carmen bites down on his lip hoping not to laugh.

"Look, we're almost there," Carmen points out into the street as they reach Lincoln Center Plaza. Helen gapes out the windshield. Five minutes had passed since they got in the car, and they were already in Manhattan.

He parks the car down in a nearby garage and helps Helen out of the car. They return to the entrance and turn to the left down Amsterdam Ave.

"Is that where we're going?" She looks at him despairingly.

Carmen holds out his arm for her to take, dutifully ignoring her question. Helen reluctantly takes it as they walk up to a tinted doorway. He knocks on the door and slyly looks at her.

The uneasiness creeps into her stomach until the door opens and out pours the sound of sweeping violins and piano. Helen softens at the familiar chords. Carmen pulls her up the stairs as they make their way into the Grand Tier Restaurant.

The waiter sits them at a corner table near the glass wall. Helen can't believe her eyes as she looks out over the Lincoln Plaza. The sun washes over the tall buildings and if she tries hard enough she can just spot Broadway. She looks over the menu prices and then at Carmen. He responds to her gaping mouth with a wave of the hand.

"Whatever you wish ma chérie." His smile warms her as he returns to his browsing. Helen's nose dips back into the menu and skims over the brunch specials. She glances at the first courses and stops at the parfait.

"What would the lady like to start with?" His pen to his pad bent down to better hear Helen. He starts scratching away as she answers. "Ah very good—the berry and granola parfait." He nods and turns to ask Carmen next when Helen interrupts.

"Uhm, how strong is the mint flavor against the honey?"

Both men look at her inquisitively never before hearing someone question what they've ordered. Recovering, the waiter blinks turning full face towards the woman.

"It's very light signora I assure you. The hint of mint balances the honey nicely. My wife had it herself and she loved it." He adds hoping to squash any further questioning. Helen nods and returns to the brunch specials.

"And for you signore?" He swerves back towards Carmen awaiting his answer. He observes Carmen as he studies the prices with pressed lips. The waiter is just about to push a special when Carmen flicks his hand.

"Nothing to start, but I will order the Salmon, hold the egg plant. And to drink, we'll take the Chateau '83. We're pressed for time so please hurry."

He folds the menu and hands it back to the beaming waiter after the order was taken. Helen flips to the wine list to see just why the waiter was so giddy. Helen's mouth pops back open as she spies the Château Latour Pauillac 1983 for $795.

Whether that's for a glass or the bottle Helen isn't sure but she knew that it was more than both their orders combined.

81

No wonder the jittery man is so giddy, he sniffs a big tip. He genuflects and turns to Helen one last time.

"Do you perhaps know already what you would like to follow with signora?"

He grins encouragingly. Helen glances at him and then back down quickly scanning the brunches. She spots something familiar and orders.

"Ah yes the Amarone Wine Glazed Chicken. Would you care to know how it's prepared?" He adds sarcastically and Helen eyes him.

"No, I trust it will be delicious." Helen throws back with a smile. Catching the undertone he bows and leaves the table. Helen sighs as she finally looks around her.

The breath taking view of the black set tables and red carpets follow through with hints of gold and maroon everywhere. The lighting set at candlelight.

She smiles to herself thinking back on Chad. He's probably never even seen the inside of something half as grand as this. Images of the Ritz start to creep into her head and Helen grabs for the napkin and begins to fidget with it.

After a few moments of stress relief she looks up to see Carmen. She drops the napkin and smiles. Absently she fidgets with the necklace as his gaze deepens.

"What?" She finally says agitated by his silence. He shakes his head, a smile playing on his gorgeous lips. Helen couldn't help but notice his resemblance to a pale Greek god in the flickering candle.

"Nothing... I just want to remember the way you look right now. You are so beautiful."

His eyes gleam as they fall over Helen's bodice. She crimsons as Carmen makes his way back to her face. He can't help but melt at Helen's rising blush.

He leans over the table hovering over the candles. Helen sighs as he comes closer and reaches for her hands. Hands clasped they stare unabashedly forgetting themselves, as the waiter shows up with her parfait.

"Oh!"

Helen jumps and drops Carmen's hands as another jittery pair places the yogurt on a plate before her. She places her hands in her lap embarrassed. She peeks up at Carmen to see him smiling wickedly. Helen's eyes fall back to the berries and granola as her cheeks begin to burn.

"Does everything look good to you signora?" The waiter doops down into Helen's view and spooks her again. He grins revealing an unsightly smile. She shudders silently.

Regaining her composure she waives her hand and shakes her head, "It's just fine, thank you." She smiles hoping he'll go away. When he does she turns to Carmen and huffs. "He's creepy." Carmen chuckles at her frankness.

"I agree chérie."

Helen squints at his shaking shoulders in the flickering light. Annoyed she stabs the three layered cup with a spoon and shoves it into her mouth. Carmen stops laughing as he spots vanilla yogurt on the corner of her mouth. He taps his finger to his mouth gesturing towards her.

Carmen can't help letting his mind wander to what else the white yogurt could be. Embarrassed he erases the thought as Helen finally wipes the smear off. Helen hopes it didn't look like a glob of—

Helen is startled to see the creepy man by their table again after the inappropriate thoughts jumped into view. Carmen takes in her wide eyed expression and mistakes it for her agitation with the waiter. After he places their entrees on the table Carmen stops him and whispers in his ears.

The frightening grin returns as he takes a $100 bill from the gentleman. As he saunters off Helen watches Carmen return his wallet. "Should I even ask?" She points away from the table. The waiter slinks off to the back giddily.

"I figured you were bothered by him, so I made him go away." Carmen picks up his silver wear and cuts into his fish. Helen wrings her head dismissing the incident. She cuts into her chicken and samples it.

"Mmm!" She exclaims, savoring the flavor.

"Oh my God, that's good!" She pops another piece into her mouth letting it slide over her tongue and back. Carmen raises an eyebrow as he watches Helen shift in her chair. Carmen flushes at the thought and clears his throat.

"Are you enjoying yourself Helen?" His voice rises in the abrupt inflection. He clears his throat again attempting to rough it up. She snaps over to him entering back into reality.

Her legs unclench and she shifts forward in her seat to better look at her partner. Hair curtains her face as she plunges into shame.

"It's alright chérie, no one sees you. It's too dark in here." He winks at her.

Helen unmoved strokes back her hair and tucks it behind both ears. She forks her poultry in silence, her eyes not leaving the plate.

Carmen chuckles but quiets as his face falls with the realization he won't be able to watch Helen fully enjoy her meal anymore. Silence falls on the couple as they absently partake.

Her eyes fall onto the corked wine on ice. She could've sworn it hadn't been there moments ago. Looking out into the main dining area she searches for the deliverer, but fails to spot him. The silver eyed beauty looks over at Helen only to see her gaze drop back to the bottle.

"May I?"

He gestures towards it. She nods timidly and Carmen pulls the '83 from the ice and pours them both a glass.

"Cheers." He clinks his glass to hers. Helen's eyes drift to the floor as she sips, unnerved by Carmen's smoldering gaze hovering above the rim of his glass. Someone needs to break the growing silence but neither is willing.

Carmen returns to his plate pushing around the chewed bones. Helen looks down at her half eaten meal, and with disgust pushes it away.

She pours another glass of wine and finally clears her throat. Carmen looks up at her in mid scrape of his plate, to see what the matter is.

"Seeing as we're drinking and not toasting, I propose we make one now."

"A toast to what?"

Carmen smiles as he raises his glass in the air next to hers. He watches as Helen mulls it over. His eyes tracing over her lips as she chews on them in thought. Helen looks up to see a patient gleam in his eye.

Her confidence swells once again and before she knows it she bursts, "To love!"

Carmen's eyes start with surprise. He hadn't expected that even though they had been dating almost a year, neither of them had dared to say it to each other. At least not out loud.

"To true love!" He adds and smiles as their glasses meet together in celebration. The smile doesn't leave as they both set their glasses back down on the white linen table.

He clasps his hands before him and rests his elbows on the table ready to gaze at Helen once more. The afternoon sun beams down and glints of his watch. Distracted he looks to it and swears softly.

"Uh, chérie, we have to get going." He places a small wad of cash onto the table and helps Helen to her feet.

"What? Where are we going?"

She stumbles back to grab her purse off the table and Carmen takes her hand once more and pulls her to the exit. Confused Helen trudges down the stairs and out onto the street.

"What's wrong?"

"It's almost three!" Carmen cries as he rushes the two of them back to the garage. Impatient, he breaks out into a sprint towards the car.

Helen blinks as she watches her boyfriend disappear around the corner. She begins to take her heels off to follow him when she hears the engine of the Jag roar around the corner. Her hand stops at her shoe as she's greeted by a black mechanical monster that stops dead in front of her.

"Come on!"

Carmen yells from the window. Startled, Helen puts her foot down to the cement and bounces over to the passenger. As soon as the door is closed, she lunges deep into the seat before she can reach for her seatbelt.

When the speed lowers as they climb back onto the street she reaches for it frantically and clicks into place. She eyes Carmen wickedly putting on her shoe.

"In a rush much?" She inquires acidly.

The raven haired Adonis glances at her and then back at traffic as he tries to make his way back to the Lincoln Plaza. The slow push and pull of traffic frustrates him into near defeat. His shoulders slump as the hour reaches 2:45pm. They were never going to make it in time and all his planning would've been for nothing.

When the light finally turns green Carmen mashes the pedal and weaves in front of the slower cars leaving behind a trail of blaring horns and angry shouting. He grins to himself as he maneuvers into the plaza just minutes later. He reaches into his pocket double checking the paper inside.

She's too frightened to be mad as she braces herself with every bob and weave Carmen puts the car under. Her heart skitters as the black monster swerves around the corner and into what seems to be a large shopping center.

The car stops and Helen catches her breath and tries to calm. Her heart slows just long enough for a man to open up her door and yank her out of the seat, sending her heart sky rocketing.

Helen clamps a hand to her chest as she's pulled up cement blocked stairs and through glass doors. Her hair falls in tussled tresses into her face as Carmen lets go of her and murmurs to a man in front of them.

Sweeping back her hair, the flustered beauty looks around her and tries to clear her head. Her heart jumps as she's grabbed again but this time gently guided up padded stairs.

Helen whips her arm out of her lover's hold and huffs. She's just about had it and goes to yell at Carmen when an elderly lady interrupts.

"Would you care for a playbill young lady?"

Helen whips around confused then embarrassed. She smoothes her hair back and accepts the bill. Taking a minute to collect herself, she looks down on the face of the pamphlet. Suddenly her eyes widened and she snaps up to find Carmen's gleaming eyes.

"How did you—?"

"Surprise!" He says raising his hands in surrender. Helen tears as she gazes once again at the cover for Tchaikovsky's Swan Lake.

Her mother had taken her to see this when she was a child. It was the only time she really bonded with her, and because of it she wanted to be a dancer. Little did she know, years later her mother would laugh at her dream.

Helen feels the tears fall as she recounts the memories. She didn't know she had mentioned it to Carmen. That she couldn't quite remember. She wipes her face as they shuffle forward.

They hustle inside the Koch Theatre to claim their seats. Helen looks at her lover adoringly and asks, "How did you know this was my favorite ballet?"

She holds up the playbill in front of her waiting. Carmen gently scoots her into the orchestra center and into row E. As they settle into seats 116 and 117 he finally turns to Helen to answer her.

"Lucky guess?"

Helen eyes him suspiciously but doesn't say a word.

"What? It was the only thing decent that was playing on Valentine's Day. I wanted today to be perfect for you."

He feathers the slipper necklace resting on her left breast. She sighs beneath his touch. When her head stops spinning she looks into his eyes.

"This was the first ballet I ever saw. It was the only one my mother took me to see before she dedicated her life to the institute." Helen frowns, but moves on, "The Swan Princess is the reason why I had wanted to become a ballerina as a little girl..."

She smiles tearfully at him. Her eyes softly close as his hand reaches to cup her face. Her heart jumps delightedly as she feels the soft lips of her boyfriend's lovingly caress hers.

Helen reaches up to his face and pulls Carmen tighter deepening the kiss. Dizziness sweeps over her as the room begins to spin and she's out of air. Breaking the kiss she draws in a deep breath filling her breasts.

She moves in to continue the embrace when Carmen holds her face and whispers softly, "Happy Valentine's Day Helen. I love you." Helen stops and looks at him as if for the first time and new tears spring down her face.

90

She hadn't expected him to say anything and here he had just said it as if on cue. Sputtering softly his ivory goddess tries to quiet herself. He cups her face and draws her closer to look deep into her eyes as the tears stream down her face. Finally, his Venus speaks.

"I love you..." She breathes as he holds her captive. Satisfied her prince kisses the top of her head and pulls her close securing her beneath his arm.

Just then the dimming light signals the ballet will begin. Helen snuggles deeply into her man's arms as he squeezes her gently to him. She closes her eyes in quiet prayer thanking God for the bit of happiness that came into her life.

"Let's relax and enjoy ma fifille, it's about to begin."

He nestles his chin into her soft hair and she melts into his side further. What could be more perfect? She wonders, but before she can come up with anything, the curtain rises revealing the arresting sounds of the orchestra and the dark stage.

And upon there she laid eyes on the ballerina who captivated her all those years ago. Helen watches as she pirouettes across the stage until the villainous sorcerer comes to prey upon her. She watches as he chases her about the stage and eventually turns her into the swan.

As the scene changes, Helen eyes Prince Siegfried in his grand birthday party strutting about the stage mingling with his guests. It's not too long after, that his mother gives him his bow, a symbol of coming of age and his quest of manhood.

Helen sighs as she thinks of how soon the Prince will finally come upon the lake, meeting his love for the first time. A beautiful swan floating up to him at the bank side named Odette. Helen can't help it even though she knows what's going to happen; she cries.

Her mind drifts thinking of Carmen as Siegfried and her as his beloved Odette. What if someone came to take him away from her? Who would want to break them apart in the first place, and cause them pain and misery? Who would be that evil?

Snapping from the image, she turns behind her to see a voluptuous blond causing a stir with the man next to her. Helen glares at her in the dark. How can someone be so tasteless?

She shivers in spite of herself when the sudden resemblance between the woman and her ex's wife suddenly appears. The woman looks at Helen pointedly, making her uneasy and eventually turning around. She laughs as Helen sulks forward.

"That woman behind us is so rude!" She whispers seething at Carmen. She clutches his arm to calm herself. He pats her and continues to watch the lovers dance about on stage. It isn't until the blond right behind him giggles loudly that he turns around.

"Excuse me madam, but would you please be so kind as to keep it down? We're trying to enjoy the ballet." Carmen sweetly adds, but to no avail.

In the dark he sees the outline of a frown as the woman stares at him in silence. Unnerved by her icy stare, he curtly nods and faces forward. A shiver trails down his spine in spite of himself when the woman leans forward.

"I'll quiet down, Carmen." She leans back and laughs softly.

His blood runs cold with the recognition of her voice. He shifts in his chair, acutely aware now of the woman in the row behind them. Not knowing what to do next, Carmen just stays put wrapping his arm tighter around Helen. Shit. How did she know he was here? Carmen shakes his head absently. No. The important question is does anybody else know?

Chapter 7

Carmen's eyes shift as he clutches Helen to his side during the intermission. They walk up to the bar only to find themselves in a line. Thank God neither of them is thirsty enough to complain. Carmen scans the crowd looking out for the woman and squeezes Helen closer.

He hisses when he sees the top of a blond head and moves Helen behind him. Relief floods Carmen as the strange skinny blond walks by. Helen looks at her boyfriend, worried. After being swung back and forth she needs to know what's up with him tonight.

"What's got you on edge? You've been like this since we left from lunch."

Carmen looks down to meet Helen's gaze and hesitates. What made him anxious early was nothing in comparison to the shit storm he was bracing for. What could he say to her?

Little did she know, that the earlier excitement was out of lateness for the ballet, but now... Carmen's teeth set on edge grind together as he scans again. When they reach the bartender, Carmen's all nerves.

"Scotch on the rocks." He quickly turns towards the crowd not wanting to be taken unawares. Helen looks at him queerly and adds her order for a chocolate martini. The

94

bartender nods and goes to work. Whilst the drinks are being made, Helen tugs on his arm impatiently.

"Honey what's wrong?"

She implores, but to no avail. Carmen smiles at her reassuringly and then snaps up looking out into the crowd. Frustrated, she tries to follow his gaze but doesn't see anything. She huffs and turns to pick up her drink and jabs Carmen to do the same.

After he pays, they walk over to a nearby table to finish their drinks. Helen stares at him stirring her martini around. What has gotten into him? I've never seen him so- on edge before.

Just as she's about to inquire again the sound of a bell softly tolls, signaling five minutes remain. She gulps down the rest of her drink and goes to return it to the counter, when Carmen pulls her by the arm and swiftly re-enters the theatre.

The blond woman Carmen had been looking for spotted him and smiled. She arched her eyebrow as he saw her in return. Her lips curled up menacingly as Carmen grabbed his date by the arm and pulled her into the crowd. The woman sighs and follows after the sounding bell. She snaps her fingers to signal her date and he appears with a shrimp hanging from his mouth.

"You idiot!"

She croons and sighs rolling her eyes as she drags him back to their seats.

Carmen leaps down the stairs with Helen trailing behind her looking for their seats. As he spots them he whirls her around until she's sitting right next to him. His arm arches over her shoulder and brings her in closer. Suddenly claustrophobic Helen pulls out from under him and gives him a dirty look.

"You better answer me right now!" She demands folding her arms. Carmen looks at her imploringly, but it's the dimming lights that save him.

"Shh, chérie, act two is about to start." Just as Helen's about to complain, he drags her back under his arm and hushes her. The lights dim and the curtains rise to a twilight stage as Siegfried finds his way to Swan Lake. He wanders around hunting, unaware of the sorcerer. To his amazement a beautiful swan dances up to him and he is entranced.

But the swan turns human as night falls and she tells the Prince that she is Odette, the Swan Queen. Siegfried is warned that she has been put under a terrible curse by an evil sorcerer, but before they can try to break the spell, the villain appears whisking her away.

A flood of swan princesses fill the lake in a beautiful dance scene to beguile and throw off the Prince. He can't follow if he doesn't know where she is.

Helen's mind drifts back to her day dream watching Carmen try to chase after her but is thwarted by a blond sorceress... A gut feeling creeps up, and Helen darts a glance in the cover of her hair at the blond in F 118.

96

Evelyn sneers back at Helen as she catches her eye. What an airhead! She scoffs. Evey shoves the goon next to her and he snorts awake. She rolls her eyes and returns her attention to the ballet. What luck that she was able to locate Carmen in such a timely manner!

And to see that he's found himself a lovely tart as well. Jealousy pangs Evelyn as she eyes the little brunette again. Carmen was hers and hers alone. He did whatever she said and she loved it. She loved him and that was a first.

Evey didn't "love" anything. Pity though that he wanted to leave her. Leave the family. And yet she thought things were going so well, and then he had to ruin the fun. Evelyn pouts as she remembers their last encounter.

Carmen decided he didn't want to be a criminal anymore, even though it had made him considerably rich. Evelyn had pleaded with him to stay with her, to take the place of their "father".

Their leader had recently died in their latest heist. He had gotten too greedy, and with all fat pigs he was slaughtered for it.

Carmen was beholden to the man who took him off the streets of Marseilles. To Carmen the man was a father. So, upon his untimely death, Carmen wanted nothing more to do with the voleurs. In his bitter rage, he renounced his role to take over the clan and decided to leave for America.

Evelyn sharply reminded him that he couldn't just leave. There were consequences to leaving the family on such bad terms. She told him he must make it fair. In the old tradition, it was blood in and blood out. With a curt nod, the weary young man gave his consent.

97

That following night, Evelyn brought her chosen opponent for Carmen. The brother of her Valentine's date was a burly man who had a scar under his right eye that reached the tip of his mouth. He ran a hand over his shaved head as he approached the 20 year old boy.

The rest of the group gathered around in a ring as the two fighters commenced their dance. Shouts and jeers were heard as the Goliath leapt after Carmen with his blade.

He missed as the youth skipped out of the way and followed through with a slice to the man's back. A guttural cry wrenched through the air as the fighter arched in surprise. Carmen danced back around the circle keeping a wary eye on his opponent.

The boar of a man lurched forward and started for him again. Carmen side stepped falling out of the attacker's line of approach. The goon counteracted matching the boy step for step.

The boy saw his next move before he did it and anticipated the lunge. In a flash the boar charged for him. He jumped out of the way, spun on his heels and landed his dagger into the spine of his attacker.

Driving it deeper in, Carmen plunged his blade forcing the man to fall to the ground. As the man died, Carmen relinquished his weapon and wiped it clean. Out of breath, he wiped his brow and looked into the crowd. Somewhere between the lunge and the counter attack they had fallen silent.

A scream pierced through the air as Evelyn sailed forward and slashed at Carmen in rage. Alert at the sound, he turns to face it. Taken off guard, the boy threw his hand with the blade up to protect himself. Flesh tore as the metal met his skin and ran down his arm. He jumped to his feet as he knocked his lover to the ground.

Evelyn gasped as the favor was returned and Carmen's dagger pointed in her face. Her eyes trailed from the steel up to its owner in horror. She whimpered defenseless, as Carmen held her at knife point, his eyes hard as the steel he wielded. Evelyn met his gaze with defiance and spat at him. His eyes didn't waiver as it landed at his feet.

As a last resort Evelyn beseeched her lover. "Carmen, don't do this. You love me." She cried.

Not moving an inch Carmen replied, "You're the devil!"

Evelyn's eyes peeled at him in response, her anger flaring. She struggled to get to her feet but couldn't as the blade neared her throat.

"Don't move!"

The crowd around them grew restless as they watched their prospective leader and his queen in a lovers' quarrel. Confusion swept over as the realization that the couple was no more, set in.

Evelyn looked to them in desperation. But, no one dared to move against Carmen after witnessing him take down their strongest fighter. Infuriated, Evelyn let out a roar and faced him once again.

"Are you going to kill me, Carmen?"

Her accent lilting as she taunted her companion. She gifted him a devilish smile as she looked from blade to man. Carmen didn't hesitate as she gave him her signature seduction, but instead grimaced. She frowned, seeing she no longer had a hold.

"Can I get up now?"

She waited as he hovered away from her, allowing her to get to her feet. "Merçi." She acidly thanked. Brushing herself off and tucking the few out of place hairs she turned away from Carmen.

He hesitated but then sheathed his blade as he watched her turn on him and toward the crowd. He leapt back as she came back with her blade in hand aiming for his chest. Catching Evelyn, he shook the knife from her hand and wrenched her arm behind her back. She cried out in pain as he pulled tighter.

"That wasn't very smart, my pet." He hissed into her ear.

She growled at her captor as she struggled to break free. Evelyn cried out again as pain met her attempt once again.

"I wouldn't do that if I were you chérie. Now this is what you are going to do. You are going to watch me leave but you are NOT to follow, crompenez?"

When Evelyn didn't answer fast enough he wrenched her arm higher. She screamed and nodded her head. When she still didn't answer he jerked her backward.

"Yes! Yes I hear you, ok! Let me go Carmen! You're hurting me!" She pouted.

Satisfied she had no other weapons on her; he waited a few moments longer to see if there was anything else she wanted to pull. After a few minutes, he let her go. Evelyn tumbled forward as he released her arm. Wounded, she grabbed her arm and nursed it. She glared at him with murderous rage.

She would make sure one day to return the favor. Carmen stared at her as well gauging and anticipating her next move. When she finally gave up trying to stop him, he went back inside the maison and grabbed his bag.

He walked out to find the crowd was no longer in a circle but scattered about watching him as he reached the hidden drive way. In the middle, was Evey watching with scorn as he made his way to a nearby stolen car.

Her eyes followed until the car disappeared around the corner and into the night. She made a vow that one day she would see him again. Next time, he would be the one wounded, and humiliated.

Two years after he left, Evelyn was leading the family in his place. She had changed everything around. She cut off old business relationships and led the family toward drug dealing and black market arms deals. Some of the members began to question Evey's judgment as the body count rose.

She was reckless and she didn't care. Her mind was consumed by her vendetta; her anger driving them further into hard crime. They knew she was in over her head when she began taking the drugs meant to be sold. After three years had gone by, the crew was getting fed up with her bull shit. Some wanted out, while others wanted Evey gone.

When finally confronted, Evelyn sneered at the voleurs and dared any of them to take her on. But seeing the hurt in her eyes, and the erratic movement in her arms, they simply stood and waited.

Defeated, she dropped her knife and her gaze followed. She looked about her for any sympathizers, only to once again be met with indifference. How would she get Carmen back now without the family behind her?

She forced the gang to accept her conditions before stepping down. Just a few more thousand dollars and she would leave without any trouble. And in her cunning, Evey made her last deal with a client she had persuaded to join her in America.

Once landed, she traveled to the heart of New York City to reestablish her narcotic business. With the new client in hand, Evey ventured out to a wider client base on the main streets of Queens and Brooklyn. After about a year, she had established her own "cartel". Once or twice, police had almost come across her in the middle of a transaction.

Realizing it was getting too risky and a bit naïve to sell right on the streets, she and her client turned partner created a local night club.

Set in the outskirts of Soho, the night club grew a fast underground reputation. As the business grew, Evey's anger cooled. The club was her priority now. Each night, she stood in her office overlooking the dancers and junkies on the floor. She smiled at her handiwork, gloating.

102

That's when she spotted him. The delicious blonde was standing at the bar. It had been awhile and Evey was more than interested. Making her way down to the main floor, she eyed him catching his attention. He smiled but nervously looked around, wondering who she was looking at. When it was made clear it was him, Chad moved to meet her on the dance floor.

He hadn't been getting anything out of Helen for the past three months. In fact, it was kind of a dead relationship anyway. So, when Evey came to him that night, he was more than willing to forget her. They swayed on the dance floor. The pulse of the house music driving them further into each other's arms. Heat rose between them as the tempo picked up.

Evey signaled to move off the dance floor. The both of them sweaty and parched. They ordered drinks as they sat at the bar. When the music slowed, she asked a question.

"Oh no," he put his drink down, "this is my first time here. Yeah, my best friend, he uh—told me about it. 'Said I should come." He tried for another sip.

"Is your friend here tonight?" Evey leaned forward distracting the boy. She cleared her throat to get his attention.

"Oh, what? Uh, no he's not. He's back at the dorm, studying."

"You're in college?" She raised an eyebrow. She sat back waiting for the cub to answer.

"Yeah, St. John's." He threw back the rest of his drink.

"What's your name?" She yelled as the music begun to pick up. They scooted closer to better hear the other.

"Chad!" He hollered back.

She stuck her hand out, "Evey." They shook hands. She lingered, tracing her fingers over the back of his hand. Chad looked down at her fingers and gulped.

He snapped up when she spoke again. Missing what she said, he asked her to repeat it.

"Do you have a girlfriend', I said."

Chad hesitated, not knowing quite what to say. He grimaced to himself, and then looked to Evey. "Yeah, I guess you can say that." He shyly smiled up at her.

"Really," she purred. Perfect. Just what she needed. What was life without a beautiful distraction? And he was beautiful.

When Chad saw she hadn't run away, he perked up. Maybe this could work for him. He finally put down his glass and moved towards Evey's ear.

"—But it's nothing serious."

She pulled back in surprise and looked at the youth. They locked eyes.

Evelyn felt something of her old self slip back in. She grabbed his hand and led him across the dance floor. They went up the stairs and into her office. The door closed and the pair crashed into each other, tearing at their clothes.

The following nights, Chad would meet Evey at the club once Helen was asleep. She was never the wiser, as he crept out and returned early in the morning.

He couldn't believe his friend was right about that club! And to think, he almost married Helen after all! Nah, she wasn't the one for him. Evey, now she was the woman of his dreams.

She was older, had money, sexy as hell, and they never got bored. Chad thought of all the times he and Helen had sat on the couch, watching Kitchen Nightmares and re-runs of My Fair Wedding.

A few months down the road, Chad was head over heels. He hadn't the nerve to tell Helen yet, but who cared? Nothing worried him as long as he was with his sugar mama. Eventually, her office became too cramped, so Evelyn decided to move their party to a hotel room far from the club.

She had hoped that being under a new man would make her forget about the old one. She couldn't be more wrong. At first, she was only interested in fun and something to do while her club took off. It wasn't until Chad gurgled "I love you" in a post coital stupor, that she thought of Carmen.

Evelyn heaved off the slumbering college kid. She walked over to the window and drew back the curtain. Looking out into the city, Evey wondered where he could be.

"Where are you my love," she whispered into the window. She closed her eyes, reminiscing of the love she shared once with him. Tears betrayed her as they fell down her face. Angrily, she wiped them away. She moved away from the window and sat on the edge of the bed.

Spotting Chad's pack of Slims, she snagged one and lit it. She threw down the pack and looked over to see him snoring. Rolling her eyes, Evey took a drag and huffed. What the hell was she doing? She came here for Carmen, not some bum adulterer.

Taking another look at the boy, Evelyn peeled her eyes in concentration. Maybe, this could work. She loved a good arm candy and he would do just fine. She'd play house for now. But something was still amiss. She rubbed at her arm absently. Her face fell, recalling the last night she had seen Carmen.

A sudden flash of him holding her tight; their eyes locked in mutual hatred. She took in a breath at the memory, furious. Even if she did love him, he still broke her heart. And that did not sit well with her.

Chapter 8

Evelyn shifts in her seat as the phantom pain of her arm comes back to her. She focuses on the present to see the play coming to an end. Her date had fallen asleep again, and she jabs him upright. He snorts and wipes his face and looks over at her. She sighs in disgust, and turns to watch Carmen pull his squeeze closer to him as he quickly made his exit from the theatre. Evey smiles wickedly as he glances her way briefly, and continues up the steps. This was going to be fun. She was going to enjoy every bit of it.

"Come on!" She roughly rouses her date to his feet. She yanks his arm as they step out into the aisle and made their way back up the steps and out into the open lobby.

Helen hesitates as they walk through the exit.

"Carmen?"

In mid stride he halts and turns to his frightened companion. He slows, his grimace melting into a soft sadness. "You know that woman don't you?" Her confidence rings out, as Carmen hardens in response to the question.

She steps closer to him and looks him in the eyes. Shamefully he glances away. Helen grabs his face and makes him look at her. The boldness in her act surprises Carmen and his eyes flash an emotion Helen can't quite catch, but then it's gone and his reserve returns. His eyes dart about as a crowd of people pass them on the steps.

"Yes, I knew her. Please, Helen I will explain later, but we must leave now!" Carmen pulls her forward only to be met with resistance. Irritated, he turns and sighs. "Helen please you have to trust me now!"

"Trust you? Trust you! I've done nothing BUT trust this entire time! Who is she Carmen? Is she an old girlfriend?"

Carmen huffs, pacing up and down the sidewalk. Warily, he looks around to see if Evelyn had come out yet. Helen watches the jungle cat pace back and forth as if caged by her questions. Why is he so upset? Slamming her hands on her hips she waits for an answer.

When Carmen stalls, she huffs and steps out in front of his path. Startled, Carmen almost knocks her over. He grabs her from falling and brushes her hemline off. Helen pushes his hands away in frustration.

"Can you please answer me?!" Carmen opens his mouth-

"I can answer for you."

A lilting old French accent reaches Helen's ears and she turns to see the blond beauty walking down towards them.

She watches Evey's escort stumble about trying to keep up. Evelyn sneers at him, and he straightens up as they come to a stop. She chuckles softly as she watches Carmen stiffen and pull Helen closer. His mouth firmly sets in a tight line. The

108

frightened little doe next to him gifts him a pathetic look. Really, what did he see in her?

Carmen instinctively grabs Helen to him, blocking her body from Evelyn's path. A small growl rips from his chest as his ex closes the distance between them.

Confused, Helen looks from her boyfriend to the eerily familiar woman standing before her. She peers at Evelyn as she laughs. The goon wakes from his stupor once more. He turns to Helen and grins at her in a way that sends shivers down her spine.

"Bon soirée, Carmen."

"Hello, Evelyn." He brusquely nods.

"You remember our friend?"

She gestures to the idiot standing next to her. "You killed his brother six years ago." Evelyn smiles, as the ogre's face darkens at the recollection. He curls his lip up at Carmen. A dog at bay.

"What do you want Evey?" The acid thick in his inquiry. Evelyn stifles a mirthful chuckle. She looks over at Helen. She gives her a dazzling smile. Helen flinches at her; a nauseous roll in her stomach.

"Darling, how good it is to see you... again."

The corner of her mouth pulls up higher when Carmen turns to Helen in disbelief. Helen's eyes peel to slits as the woman addresses her casually. Her teeth set on edge as a faint stirring of memories rises.

An image of a voluptuous blond with her eyes rolling in the back of her head; a certain someone's hands wrapped around her neck in ecstasy.

"...How's Chad?" She evenly replies back to the bitch. Carmen looks back and forth between both women, confused as ever. Secretly, his heart deflates as his year old suspicion of his Lady is resurrected.

"You two...know each other?" Carmen asks weakly, but his face is smooth as marble.

"Only briefly and I wouldn't call it a meet-cute." Helen answers, her mouth barely moving as her eyes never leave Evey's.

The cougar gives to a peal of laughter as she watches the emotions flit across Helen's face. Carmen turns to Helen, his eye brow raised. She sighs in response and turns to Carmen.

"I met her the night I thought my ex-boyfriend was going to propose to me." Carmen's eyes widen in surprise as his suspicion is quelched. Compassion rises in its stead. His hand gently reaches for Helen's at her side. She clasps his tightly leaning on him for strength. Their hands joined in secrecy.

"Yes, that was a delicious night I must say. I didn't think I'd ever see you again!" Another peal of laughter erupts

110

from the home wrecker. Helen fights not to flinch at the shrill sound.

"But this? This is too perfect!

—Wouldn't you agree Carmen?"

"You didn't answer my question." Helen delivers evenly trying not to cringe at an oncoming memory. Evelyn's smile fades as she turns her attention back to the plain girl standing next to her lover. No wonder Chad was so eager to leave her.

"That poor sap, well he was fun for a little while."

"—and the wedding?"

"Hmmm, the marriage was short lived." Evey tilts her head tauntingly.

Helen's eyes widened. Her eyebrow arches in question at the cryptic response. Watching Helen, Evelyn giggles maliciously at her reluctant curiosity.

"As they say, '—until death do us part."

Helen's reserve brakes as she gasps her hand flying over her mouth. She expected that she had left him home for the evening, or hell just divorced his ass; but death? That she wasn't ready for. Poor bastard, she didn't know what to feel about it. Surprisingly, she feels a little sad.

Carmen reaches for his love but thinks better of it in front of Evelyn. He sets his jaw once more facing his past, waiting for whatever was coming next.

"I'm sorry. I didn't quite catch your name...?" Evelyn chuckles at Helen's blatant snub.

"Evelyn, but you may call me Evey." She winks dubiously at the girl. "And yours mademoiselle is of course—?" The wench raises her brow as she waits to hear what name this awfully common female may have.

"Helen." Of course it is Evey muses. *So fucking plain.* She smirks at the couple, enjoying their squirms.

"Yes, lovely name—"

"Thank you," she answers sourly. Carmen squeezes her hand reassuringly. Helen faintly pulls the side of her mouth up at him.

"So what happens now—Evelyn?"

"I can't chat with an old ami? Carmen it really has been too long! We should do this again—" she wrestles her date's arm to turn and head down the street. As she walks away, she looks over her shoulder and gifts the frozen couple a pernicious smirk, "—soon."

Helen slowly turns her eyes away from the cruel woman walking down the street to face Carmen. Her eyes fall short of his gaze as it trails after Evelyn, glowering. She didn't notice until now that his teeth were clenched.

His breath seethes in and out, hissing as the air makes its escape. She gently reaches for him hoping to get his attention. He snaps towards her, his gaze cold until he regains his composure.

112

She relaxes as he softens and cups her face. Her hand reaches for the one holding her face, and pulls it to her side. They stand there contemplating their joined hands, not wanting to break the silence. But Carmen sighs and breaks it first.

"Come on." He gently escorts Helen back to the garage, where a long ride home awaited them.

The sound of belts clicking and the humming of the engine permeate through the tinted car. Helen looks out the window and into the night to take her mind off the past hour. But, even the city lights and window displays can't erase the memories of Chad, and the evil bitch that had gotten to both men.

The car glides back onto 9A as Carmen makes the turn. His eyes leave the road to glance at Helen only to find her staring out the window, seemingly calm. He swears to himself thinking of how their first Valentine's Day had gone so terribly wrong.

What had begun with a perfect evening, now ended with broken memories of the past coming back to haunt them both. The couple numbly looks out before them as they reach the valet. As they pull up, they stare out their respective windows avoiding one another.

Carmen knows he now has no other choice. She needs to know before Evelyn comes back and finds them again. And who knows what that bitch may pull the next time. Carmen shakes his head at the thought of his Goddess getting hurt. She had to be ready for whatever Evey might throw at her.

And right now, arming Helen with his past was the best he could do for now. He has to tell her about his life in France and how he had come to be the owner of such an impressive scar. It's time to tell her, who he was.

Chapter 9

Car doors slam as they make their way onto the sidewalk and into the building. Carmen can't stand the silence between them. But, with nothing to offer he sighs defeated, and calls for the elevator. Normally, their silence was jovial and welcomed, but at the moment it was strained with tension.

Helen surrounds herself with her hair, blocking herself from view. Peeking through the mousy strands to look at him, Helen wonders why he was so silent in the car. She thought for sure he would've explained on the drive over. Maybe he thought she forgot and wasn't going to tell her anyway. Helen sniffs indignant at the thought as they finally reach their floor. She steals herself ready to confront Carmen head on.

The elevator swings open and Helen shoves her way off first. She turns on her heel, arms folded to face Carmen as he steps off meekly after her. Waiting still for him to speak, she raises her eyebrow in anticipation.

He hesitates, catching her eye as he makes his way for his adjoining apartment. Furious, Helen stomps behind him and follows to his door. Throwing her hands up, she storms towards her apartment.

"Well, goodnight then!" She turns the key.

"Chérie, wait—"

The key halts as she waits to hear more. When nothing readily comes, she opens her door. Carmen grabs her arm out of desperation. Disgusted, she looks down at his hand then to his face, daring him to do anything else. He sighs, dropping his hand and backs away.

"Thank you." She swings it closed only for his arm to stop it halfway. "Oh!" She lets go of the door as it bounces back. Carmen shakes his hand trying to wring out the pain.

"Please," he beseeches, "now let me explain."

Helen takes in his sad eyes, pouty lips and all over disheveled look. Sighing, she lets him come in through the door. Damn, she was a sucker for puppy dog eyes. Wasting no time, she plops down on her sordid couch waiting for Carmen to start.

Sensing her irritation, he draws in a big breath and sits down in front of her.

"Where do I begin?"

He asks, solemnly joining his hands in front of him. He looks at Helen for help only to be met with flustered apprehension. Realizing he's getting nowhere fast he asks," What would you like to know first, Helen?"

"Let's start with Evelyn…" She says. Canting her head to the side, folding her arms in front of her; she peels her eyes at him waiting for an answer. Lost, he fumbles with his hands trying to find the right words to say.

116

"As you've guessed we were formerly together." Helen scoffs in spite of herself. Catching her own sardonic response, she readjusts her arms giving him the benefit of the doubt. Carmen looks at her, leery of the fact that this was going to be a long night.

"Back in Marseille— you can say we were perfect for each other." Carmen smiles bitterly. She flinches at Carmen's remark, not sure which way to take it.

He clears his throat, "Anyway, we were unstoppable. Nothing stood in our way. We were as you say the 'Bonnie and Clyde' of France." The smile doesn't touch his eyes for the second time. Helen's coldness melts as she shifts on the couch, wondering where Carmen's going with it. Watching his shoulders slump as he loses himself in his memories, she instinctively reaches out for him.

Thinking better of it, she retracts her hand before he lifts his head up to meet her gaze. Frozen, neither moves as they lock eyes, lost in the other's gaze. The sad bitterness of his past creeps into his stare. Helen looks away unable to bear it any longer.

"... I was a part of a—"he swallows as he notes her anticipation. Ashamed, he tries to finish, "—gang."

Helen's eyes were wide only to settle at the underwhelming confession. He was a criminal, that's the catch, she laments. Seeing her sudden change in expression, Carmen panics.

"But I got out of it! As you can see! I was an orphan. The 'family' found me and took me in. The leader, found me scrounging for food at the age of fourteen. He brought me to

117

their safe house, fed me and told me about the gang and what they do.

"At the time, it sounded so wonderful, like a fairytale come true. At last, I had finally found a home to call my own. And the man who took me in, I came to regard him as a father figure. Loved him like a father…"

Carmen pauses, the words catching at the back of his throat. When he's able to continue, he clears his throat rubbing the space between his eyes. The pain of his father's death coming back to haunt him.

"Once I had been initiated," he glances at Helen to find her once again curious. He swallows back the rising panic and ignores her unspoken questions.

"They taught me the trade, how to pick locks, hot wire cars, handle weapons, you name it. It was when I had begun to come into my own that she showed interest.

"She had always been around I realized, watching me, waiting. He noticed her watching and told me who she was. Said she was dangerous, and not to be trifled with. This only intrigued me more and my father knew he was too late.

"'I'm Evelyn, but you can call me Evey.' She said to me. I was so baffled I didn't know what to say. I was sixteen by then, and no way with women.

"Luckily, she took the lead and taught me things that Father didn't. She took me under her wing, teaching me, guiding me, and ushering me into manhood." He catches Helen stiffening at his covert confession.

"So… She was your first?"

"—Yes."

Helen slowly nods and tries not to fidget with her coat. Waiting for him to continue she tries to block out visions of

118

Evelyn beneath Carmen. She swallows back the bile as Carmen moves to speak, thankful for the distraction.

"She had made me hers, and we sought out trouble just for sport. She would set up the job, baiting the lonely guy on the street or making her way into a family's household—"Carmen trails off noting Helen's expression.

She tries not to cringe as she crosses her legs. Not wanting his past to intrude on their future, Helen fights the disgusted feeling creeping in as she closes up against their love affair. Her face grimaces as her insecurity leads her to regret all the nights they shared the past year.

Carmen's arms reach for Helen only to hang in the air. Slowly, he retracts them and falls back into the opposing love seat. His hands nervously slip beneath his thighs. Thinking for sure that he's lost his love to his unforgiving words, Carmen falls silent.

Watching contemptuously his hands drop away from her guarding arms, Helen feels even more vulnerable and upset. She shifts a little looking at Carmen. Was that the end of his explanation? If it was, it was a shitty one. Helen's met with a nagging silence as Carmen sits crestfallen.

"So what then?" She begrudgingly asks. Her arms falter as Carmen lifts his head weakly to look at her. Her anger waivers as she sees the defeat in his eyes. Forcing her chin up, Helen arches a brow in question waiting for him to finish his life story.

She wanted to cut him a break but Helen had done enough of that in the past, and look where it led her. Sitting upright, her eyes demand him to continue.

But Carmen's at a loss. He looks miserably at Helen. What could she possibly want to know after knowing about his and Evey's past? His hands come out from under him, palms out in surrender. What do you want me to say chérie? When she doesn't answer, he looks about the room exasperated.

What can he possibly do to save not only this conversation, but the future of this relationship? Absently he scratches at his scar. Helen's eyes fall to where his hand touches his arm. He casually drops his hand not acknowledging her curious stare. Carmen plays it cool as he happens upon a potential save.

"—and, then one day I wanted out. Not even Evey's purrs could hold me there any longer," he ignores Helen's tightened face.

"The last time I saw her we had had a fight. Not an argument, we both at one time had a knife at the other's back." Helen's face softens into a smug blank expression. Carmen dutifully ignores it, not letting it distract him.

"You see, in order to leave the—in order to leave you had to combat the best fighter at the time. Very old fashioned. The gentleman you met this evening—" Helen snorts at the word choice

"—was the brother of the knifeman I was up against. He was a great deal bigger than his younger counterpart, but I was faster. Where he had brute strength I had skill. He was no match for my quick thinking and agility—" She gifts him a look that makes him clear his throat.

120

Helen can't help but give him a look. What was it with testosterone? Men, she rolls her eyes and waits for him to continue. She shifts herself re-crossing her legs. They begin to fall asleep, but she's too stubborn to unclench her body and relax against the security of her worn in couch.

Immaturity makes her fidget with her arms. She tries to keep them steady. But, as she feels her reserve slip and her anger fade, she finds it difficult to keep the stubborn position any longer.

"Evey had picked him to fight me. In all the time of her teaching, she neglected to learn me in the ways of self defense.

"She needn't bother though, for I had had ample practice from father as well as other experienced fighters. Including the opponent I was facing that night.

Carmen's face falls lost in thought again. Flashes of the fight clamor through his head. He remembers the tight grip of the blade; his sweat stinging his eyes, the adrenaline that coursed through his veins.

Helen stares at him wondering what happened that's making him daze out like this. She starts to worry as his emotions shift and change across his face. A kaleidoscope of unexplained expressions.

He catches himself when he surfaces to Helen gawking at him in question. Clearing his throat, he tries to recall the thread of conversation before he drifted off. Grappling for words, he absently looks around himself as if to find them on the floor. Carmen spares a quick glance only to catch her losing interest.

Defeated he asks," I'm sorry. Where was I?"

Annoyed, she squirms around on the cushions. Helen softens as she looks at his scar again. Sighing, she drops her stiff shoulders, "Evelyn wasn't the one to teach you so she thought you would lose against her guy." Her arms follow suit as she tucks her palms beneath her lap.

Carmen sweeps a hand across his tumbling hair and chuckles bitterly. "I didn't say she believed I would lose."

He looks up at her, cocking an eyebrow. She stares back challengingly. Her arms resume their position in front of her chest. Her legs cross stiffly.

"It was implied."

She throws back with more intensity than she intended. Not backing down, she holds the pose until Carmen chuckles again. Helen falters at the sound but pulls herself together as he clears his tickling throat.

"Ok…Well, we were fixed in the center of the circle of the growing crowd. His butterfly knife out by his side never had the pleasure of drawing blood. My knife was simpler but had seen more fights than his shiny new gift from Evey.

"I broke a sweat, yes, but he, in the end, was bested by my rusted blade.

"Evelyn was furious; she leapt at me as I turned to leave—"

Helen draws in a sharp breath. Her hands gripping the cushions, unaware they were no longer tucked beneath her chest.

Catching this, Carmen pauses with concern. He looks her over until his eyes lock on hers. She blinks and slowly exhales as she unclenches. Swallowing back her embarrassment she looks at him to continue. They both shift uncomfortably.

"She had knocked me down out of surprise. When Evelyn went to strike again, I threw my arm up—" he pulls down his sleeve, "— out of instinct. She left a nasty scar but it bought me enough time to gain the upper hand.

"And once I had it, I made sure my point was made very clear. She will claim to this day that I broke her arm and giving her chronic pain, but I know better.

"It seemed pain was the only thing Evey understood— understands. It was the only way I could ensure my safety and leave that place for good.

"So even though I now have to cover this up, it will always be a reminder of what I'm willing to do, to sacrifice to get what I want." He slowly lifts his cool gray eyes up at Helen and she stifles a gasp.

Did he just imply that that's what he would do for me? Impossible, she thought. Why would he risk his life for someone he barely knew for a year? Suddenly, Helen feels uncomfortable all over again.

Seeing an opening, Carmen moves off his couch to slide next to Helen. She shifts away rather than closer, but he chooses to ignore it.

123

"Chérie, I want you to know that all of that is behind me. She is my past, and even though she is here again now, does not mean she will be in my future."

Hesitantly, he grabs for her hand. Her eyes fall to their clasp and she absently frowns. Was she really worried that this bitch would come back only to take him away now, and finish what they started? Timidly, she pulls her hand back and fidgets with her hair.

Carmen's confidence waivers as he looks down at his empty hand once again. What was it going to take for her to trust him? Would she ever? Trying not to panic, he looks up at her searching for some kind of answer.

Her eyes quickly shift away and over at nothing on the wall. He sighs as the hopelessness sinks in. Carmen turns to move off the couch and take his leave for good.

"So… You're not a vampire…" Helen says smoothly to lighten the mood.

He turns slowly back around to look to see if she's serious. When all he's met with is a blank stare, he puzzles. Wait, did she really think I was the undead? Slowly, he steps forward trying to make sense of what she had just said.

"E—excuse me?"

Helen raises her eyebrows in response. No way is she going to crack now, this was too good. She was joking at first, but the way he responded made her re-think whether or not it could be true. His clear look of shock has her thrown not giving her much to go by. So she goes with a slightly less obvious yet reasonable feature that seemed "vampire like".

"Your eyes. They're an unnatural shade of gray. Almost silver."

Carmen tips his chin up in defiance. His eyes, he thought, were what made him unique. And well, to be honest what drew most women in. Was that the reason why?

Because they thought I might sparkle in the sunlight? Or drink their blood? Instantly, Carmen resents today's pop culture, and how out of control it has gotten with the idea of the supernatural.

"Plus your skin is pale white. And your hair is really shiny and dark—"

"Stop! Please." He throws his hand out in defense flinching at the replay of the cliché paranormal romance scene.

Helen stops, her mouth open in mid sentence. Realizing how dumb she looks and pops it closed. Carmen rubs between his eyes trying to massage out the irritation this whole situation's bringing him.

Confused, Helen waits to see if she took it too far, or if he is struggling to tell her some truth. She leans forward trying to will the answers out of him, but to no avail. He's still rubbing his head.

Great, she thought, I've pissed him off. If he is one, he'll probably eat me and get rid of the body so no one finds out.

Not finding the relief from the massage, he begins to pace in front of the table. He looks up at Helen from time to time. Finally he stops, rolls his shoulders and looks Helen dead in the eye.

"I am not a vampire. And I am a little insulted that you would make such a remark about my eyes and complexion.

"I happen to love my eyes because they are unlike any others I've seen. My skin is pale because I am European—

"—and I don't like the idea of skin cancer—and why would you think I was a vampire anyway? I have not done anything super human. Nor have I even given you any reason to fear me. So, why…"

Hearing the indignance, Helen eases back and chews her lip.

"I don't know—"she fidgets with her fingers, too embarrassed to meet his heated gaze. "Because you talk like you come from one of my favorite novels.

"And you're really hot, which makes it harder for me to believe that you would be interested in someone like me."

Carmen softens at that, hurt that she feels so insecure about herself.

The way Americans associate beauty with power and their horrendous disregard for personality and human emotion disgusted him. Stifling a rash response he waits to see if she'll continue.

126

"I was kind of joking when I asked you that. But then, you got so defensive about it. I didn't know what to believe anymore.

"The way you treat me is like out of fairy tale, and in this city that is unnatural. I guess I was just trying to rationalize why you'd want me."

"So convince yourself that I'm Nosferatu?"

Helen curtains herself in her hair. "Well you did always sit in the shady corner at the Kaffe," she weakly replies.

Carmen's mouth screws into a half smile at her logic. He shakes his head. Edging his way back over to her, he gently eases back onto the couch. His fingers lace through her hair to open the curtain surrounding her face.

"Helen, doesn't that sound just a bit crazy?" He peeks at her frown and winces, but waits patiently for her to answer. Coaxing her, he tucks the hair and trails his fingers down her cheek.

Fighting a tear, her face goes red surprised by just how embarrassed she really is. For someone who was a college student in psychology, Helen really had absurd logic and reasoning.

She pulls his hand down and tries to push the tear back. When that doesn't work, she sniffs it back, hoping to stall it from falling down. Finally, she looks at her dream guy. He smiles in encouragement.

"It does, I suppose." She finally manages resigning to wipe her face with her sleeve. Helen finds herself chuckling out of spite and Carmen along with her.

When she pulls herself together her eyes meet his more confidently. "Maybe I need to stay away from the teen section from now on." She chides herself.

Happy to see her smile and the mood lighten, he giggles touching her face again. "Maybe!" She gives him a sheepish smile and relaxes against the back of the couch.

"So what now?" The question hangs between them as their heads crush into the cushions. Carmen absently reaches for the few loose strands not caught between her cheek and the couch.

"Well, we could go see that new wizard movie. I heard it's spectacular in 3D."

Helen chuckles at his deflection, grateful that they could put this behind them for good. Mustering as much deflection as she can at the moment, Helen gives Carmen her best smolder.

"—Sounds fun."

Chapter 10

Evey checks her watch as night approaches. "Perfect," she says, right on time. She walks across the street and into the café. She had made sure that he had come by himself.

The past few months had been a pain in the ass. Between continuing her business, networking, and staff, she barely had time to keep track of Carmen.

But today he's right where she wanted him. Evey had made sure of that. It's just a matter of time, though, before that twit turns up looking for him. Her laid out plan was too perfect, almost criminal. Now, all she has to do is walk in and let the rest fall into place.

After their run in months back, Evelyn was completely ecstatic. She had found him ahead of schedule. What luck! As the valet brought her car around, she saw Carmen pull out in his Jag from the garage. She tapped her date on the shoulder when they were inside, "Follow him."

They trailed behind him as they turned down North and reached a building called Glenwood. The driver pulls over to the side. Evey looks out the window and grins. There, she saw Carmen and Helen walking silently inside. This was going to be too easy. Seeing the couple already at odds, splitting them up would be a cinch.

She walks up behind Carmen and slides her arms around his waist. Carmen jumps as he turns to find the last person he wants to see. She chuckles huskily, as she pulls back to give him space.

"What do you want Evelyn? You have to stop summoning me like this!" Carmen hisses at her. They move to the side, making way for the long line behind them.

Unnerved, Evey laughs. "What? I can't see an old boyfriend from time to time?"

"Not when I have a girlfriend waiting at home for me!" He scathes.

"What is she to you anyway? I never thought you went for girls like her."

Carmen's eyes peel at her. Through gritted teeth he exclaims, "The kind of woman who doesn't literally stab you in the back!"

"Oh come now, Carmen!" She laces her arms back around his waist, further enclosing her prey. He plucks her prying fingers from about him, and moves backward.

"Evelyn ENOUGH! What the hell do you want from me? Why are you here?!"

She clucks at him and shakes her head, scolding an unruly child. "What I want, mon chér, is you. I've come to take you back. Back to where you belong," she wraps her arms around his waist once more, "with me." She smiles seductively but to no avail. He swats her away and pulls her out of view, near the restrooms.

130

Once out of sight, he clamps his hand around her neck and pins her to the wall. Hysterical, Evey flails and scratches at his clasp trying to break free. When she realizes he's not letting up, her hands flop to her side and she huffs.

"I am NOT going back there! Do you understand me?" When she doesn't answer, he clamps down harder, choking her. "DO YOU UNDERSTAND ME?"

When she weakly nods her assent, he loosens his grip, still pinning her to the wall.

"But, I miss you Carmey..." She pouts and bats her eyelashes. Carmen flinches at the pet name, and slams her against the wall to deter further use. She wrenches at his grip.

"OW! It's true damn it! The way we left things was... not right. And you know it."

She sulks and looks at him imploringly, hoping he'll let her down. They stare at each other for a moment. Compassion overcomes Carmen, and he sighs and lets her down. Disgusted, he pushes away from her, but only enough to keep her at arm's length.

Seeing an opening, she takes it. "Come away with me. It could be like it was before Papa Maurice died. Remember?" She looks at him only to be met with stone. She bows her head in defeat.

Carmen shakes his head and moves to leave. He hears the soft cries behind him, as he moves out of the shadows and back towards the counter. He stops short but doesn't turn; not giving her the satisfaction.

"I knew you wouldn't come with me. It was hopeless to think so. I miss you, Carmen.

"And it eats me up that you are with her, and not me. Je t'aime, mon petit garçon. I never stopped loving you…"

Hearing the sincerity in her voice, he slowly turns to see if it's true. His face falls, as he looks at the total mess of the once notorious beauty he had come to love.

Evey pulls her head up to see him standing there. Hopeful, she entreats him cautiously. When he doesn't move away, she closes the distance. She stops right in front of him, holding his gaze.

"Please, give me another chance."

"You hurt me Evey. And not just with a knife—"

"I know! I know, and… I'm sorry."

Her shoulders slump with the admission. The tears spring down her face once more. She looks up at Carmen with inky eyes. He softens as the mascara runs down her face. He moves to wipe her cheeks.

"I can't live without you Carmen, mon amour!" She grabs the hand stroking her cheek, and clutches it.

"I—I've changed. You'll see! Come with me. The family misses you. When you left, everything changed! You started something!

"They wanted out too. Turn their lives around as you did!" She beams as the tears dry up. "I turned my life around, for you."

Carmen starts at her last confession. Confusions sweeps over him as the hole in his heart aches with old love. He sighs

132

torn as to what to do now that Evey had given up her old life, in the hopes of winning him back.

Frantic, Evelyn searches his face for any kind of sign. Going for it, she rushes in and pulls Carmen close. Carmen surprisingly ignites from the fiery kiss despite who it's from. Succumbing to her charms, he falls back into his old self. Eagerly, he kisses back remembering just how good it felt to be with her.

Abruptly, the moment ends at the sound of the shop bell ringing. Carmen looks up to see a shell shocked brunette standing in the doorway. As the fog clears from his head, his eyes widen with recognition.

Evey licks her lips and slowly turns to acknowledge the plain girlfriend. Again, like the devil herself, she smiles at Helen. *Gotchya.*

Helen can't believe what she's seeing. An echo of a memory mocks her as she takes in Carmen and Evey standing together in their favorite coffee shop. But instead of numb, Helen feels a burst of rage flicker deep within. The flames lick out, consuming everything in its wake.

"Helen..." Is all Carmen can manage; his heartbreaks watching hers do the same. Her breathing slows and focuses on another cheating boyfriend. Shaking her head calmly, her eyes search his. How could he, after all that's happened?

But, instead of breaking, Helen feels a steely reserve trickle through her mind. She straightens; and without wasting any more time, she curtly nods and swiftly walks back out.

He darts after her immediately, only to be pulled back. He tries to throw her off his arm, but finds Evelyn more devastated than Helen. Stopping short, he stares at her. What was he going to do now? He feels compelled to comfort Evey; yet chase after Helen.

Realizing his decision was made for him, Carmen shakes his head. His shoulders slump as he turns back to her. Evey brightens seeing that she's won. She reaches for his other arm and pulls him close.

"It's better this way, you'll see. She doesn't know you like I do mon chér. It'll be better this time." She faces him looking dead in his eyes. "I want to do right by you." She tucks her head back onto his shoulder and squeezes.

Carmen sighs as he continues to look out the window after Helen. He tears up as he reassuringly strokes Evey's hair. Carmen knew there was no getting Helen back now.

How could she even face him after what he'd done? How could he ever face her? Not after all that she had told him; and not after seeing the one person she hated kiss the man she loved.

No. It was over, and Carmen had to accept that. All he could hope for now was that one day she could forgive him. And even when that day came, would the heartbreak be as strong as it is today?

Helen walks down the street, her temples buzzing. She can't think straight with the blood throbbing in her ears. Her confident exterior gave no hint to the chaos that was brewing inside. As she reaches the corner, she takes a detour and heads to the local shop across from home. There were a few things to pick up...

Evelyn didn't think it was going to be that easy. Like stealing candy from a baby. She celebrates inside, as she continues to desperately hold onto her prize. She kisses his neck until she faces him, and plants a kiss on his cheek.

Sweetly, she suggests that they sit and chat for awhile. After being sure Carmen's convinced of her being the better choice, she offers to take him in until he can better cope on his own.

And to think, Evey muses, all she had to do was call him away from her to put this whole thing into action. After seeing him disappear into the complex, Evey pulled out her phone and texted him. She chuckled when he responded, seeing that after all these years he still had the same number.

They had met up three times before today. Each time, Evey told him to give the excuse of needing coffee. She knew eventually, if she kept him out long enough and often, Helen would get suspicious. *As insecure little girls often do.*

And like clockwork, Carmen came out to meet her only to try to tell her to go fuck herself. But, just the evidence of him showing up was proof enough he most definitely didn't mean it. Cause a little friction with the lies; endless fights about going out alone so often and voila, the perfect recipe for disaster.

Now, all she has to do was play nice for a little while. In no time, Carmen will be back to eating out of the palm of her hand. Then, all she had to do was break him and train him to oversee her club.

After all, what was a queen without her king kneeling at her side? Once situated, and eventually back in her bed, the real fun begins.

Epilogue

As the tall beautiful couple walk down the street in the setting sun, they laugh sharing an old joke. The woman's arm hooks into her lover's warming herself against the cold night air. They cross the street and head pass the Glenwood Apartments. Street lights slowly light up as they make their way down.

The building glows with the glittering lights of its tenants. The man looks up to see a shadowy figure in view. He puzzles as he peers up at the sight before him. The figure of a woman stands in the frame, holding something in her hand.

Carmen's heart breaks as he sees the vision of his former love standing four stories high. And as Evey pulls him tighter to keep walking, he eyes Helen longingly. Hoping against his better judgment that she would just happen to look down. And perhaps, hear him silently crying out for her.

The sight of his tormented Beauty would forever haunt him. Dejected, he passes the window watching the silhouette put a bottle to her mouth and swig.

Helen downs her third bottle of wine as she looks distractedly out over the city. In her drunken haze she could've sworn she saw Carmen, her ex boyfriend, walking down the street.

Curious enough, she feels nothing as she watches the figure hold onto the older blonde woman. Well whoever that is down there on the street, Helen would make sure that with the next bottle, she wouldn't remember anything.

Not even the man she had dared to love.

DEAD BODY BANKED ON HUDSON

New York, March 13, 2012
Sally Porter

A body of a Caucasian male was found early this morning by urban NY residents. Autopsy report shows an overdose on cocaine and meth. Police believe he may have been a junkie that frequented the club Pulse about 20 miles out from the victim's sighting.

The body was identified as Chad Couchon, a young business major who attended St. John's University. Found with a band on his ring finger, the male seemed to have been married as well. The police have tried to get in touch with the wife of the victim, but so far there have been no leads.

Needing confirmation of the body's identity as well as funeral arrangements, they have tried aimlessly to track her down. Fortunately, the boy's family was able to give confirmation and to collect his belongings. There will be a service held on Monday.

Police are looking for leads as to who the murder is and the trail is getting cold. One thing is for sure there are suspicions that the wife is a primary suspect. But where the bride is no one knows for sure.□

INDEX OF FRENCH TEXT

Chérie/Chér: dear

Mon Dieu: my God

Triste: sad

Après-Vous: after you

Chaque mot: every word

Voleurs: thieves, criminals

Crompenez: understand

Maison: house

Ami: friend

Mademoiselle: miss

Merçi: thank you

Ma belle fille: my beautiful "girl"

Fillfille: (baby) girl

Juste pour vous mon amour: just for you my love

Je t'aime, mon petit garçon: I love you,(boyfriend)

Mon amour: my love

Acknowledgements

To New York City I show my love for your beautiful bewitching atmosphere. I would love to acknowledge the real "Kaffe 1668", St, John's University, NYC Ballet, Grand Tier Restaurant and all the other inspiring places used in the Beloved World! I want to also show my appreciation to Rick VanMan who composed music that happens to feature on the Beloved videos and "soundtracks". Emma Enriquez your photography rocks! You always make me look good! I want to thank you and Rosanne Legon for being my two leading ladies! Rosy you're just awesome period. Jeff without you, there'd be no Carmen.

Friends and family that went through this journey with me I thank you so much! You believed me when no one knew my name. You all knew my craziness (ie."giftedness") would be good for something!

To the teachers who need to be appreciated and I would love to recognize:(Mrs.Hawes), Mr. Bogaczyk, Mrs. Herbert, Miss O'Toole, Mr. Taylor, Mr. Zayas, Miss Forte, Mr. James Sanders, and Miss Rachel Smith! Miss Smith, you were the most awesome teacher I never had! To this day I always tell people how you called me crazy for eating with chopsticks, and how you yelled to me, "Noel, get off the stage!" I'll never forget it!

To my dear friends from afar Milton Hood, Jenn Ritter, Jacco Trap, and Brittany Elizabeth I love you!

To my mother and father, no matter how you showed it, you never stopped believing that you're eccentric daughter would go far.

And to my Beloveds! Never stop believing in yourselves and in the art we make together! Keep your chin up and stay with me. There's so much more in store! I am honored and humbled to have you all with me for this ride...

©Emma Enriquez. Bleu Rose Studios

Solange believes gothic romance needs to make a true comeback. She currently is working on the next installation of the Beloved Series, Dreams of Poison. She currently lives in Virginia with her son while her husband serves in the Navy. When she's not writing, she's always behind a camera.

With music, art and her novels, she hopes to create a world in which her fans can be a part of. This is her first published novel. Check out her eBook poetry: Chocolate Roses Will I Dream, Here I Stand: In Love's Evil Embrace, and An Hour of Decadence.

Visit the World

Poetry Collections Short Stories Other Works

Catch the character bios, trailers, and music playlists

on the

Beloved World Blog, Myspace and more!

BE THE FIRST TO READ THE NEXT BOOK!

Helen and Carmen find themselves once again in a world of trouble with Evey at the helm. Evelyn's vendetta is at the heart of this sequel. With Carmen taken under by Evey, he finds himself playing a game where she knows all the rules. Will there be a second chance for Carmen and Helen? Or will everything fall apart, only for them to come so close and lose it all...

COMING 2014